# MOTHER OF WOLVES

WOLVES OF CRIMSON HOLLOW BOOK FOUR

## MICHELLE HERCULES

INFINITE SKY PUBLISHING

Mother of Wolves © 2019 by Michelle Hercules



**Editor:** Hot Tree Editing

**Photography:** Wander Aguiar

**Paperback ISBN:** 978-1-950991-70-9

PROLOGUE

GARDENS OF THE HUNTRESS – MOUNT OLYMPUS

PEGASUS HAD PROMISED HIMSELF THAT HE WOULD NEVER SET FOOT in the place, not after the humiliation he'd endured at the hands of Artemis, the proud daughter of Zeus, his master. He had been able to keep that promise for a few centuries. A blink of time for someone like him. Definitely not long enough to make him forget the pain.

He wouldn't be there if he had a choice, but refusing the request of a god wasn't something he could do, even if that god was Hades. The Lord of the Underworld had summoned him, something unexpected to Pegasus. There was no lost love between Hades and Zeus, which in consequence extended to Pegasus, being Zeus's champion and all.

Hades had a valid reason for wishing to speak to him. He had news, grave news that affected Artemis. Pegasus couldn't ignore it, even if he wished it so. Not because of Artemis—at least, that was the lie he told himself. The information Hades passed on to him would affect many lives, mortal lives. Pegasus, being one of the few immortals who still possessed a moral compass, couldn't let innocent people suffer because he was afraid to face the goddess who had mocked him after he professed his love.

Deep down, he knew his humiliation was his fault. He should have known Artemis only had eyes for her precious wolves that, in the end, forsook her for the love of a mortal woman.

Pegasus's lips curl into a satisfied grin. *As the mortals say, karma is a bitch.*

Not much has changed since the last time he visited Artemis's sanctuary. The gardens are still abundant with flowers, and the grass is soft and luscious green. Birds chirp as they fly playfully from tree branch to tree branch. In the center of the garden, the familiar white pergola with its twisty vines offers partial shade to the comfortable-looking chaise lounge Artemis prefers. However, instead of finding her lounging lazily there with a glass of red wine, he finds a woman with tangled hair sitting on the floor and cradling a large bottle of amber liquid. She's been drinking whiskey and, by her unkempt appearance, lots of it.

"Oh, look who's come to gloat," she slurs.

Pegasus stops short of stepping under the shade of the pergola. A whiff tells him Artemis has not only been drinking for quite a while, but she also hasn't bothered to bathe either. He's never seen the goddess in such a sad state.

"I didn't come here to mock your pain, but perhaps I should have come sooner. What happened to you?"

She waves her hand in a dismissive way. "Oh, nothing. Just my beloved wolves that preferred to share an insignificant mortal girl than to be with me."

Artemis has always had a flair for the dramatic. As spoiled as deities usually were, she took the grand prize as the most mercurial among them, losing only to her twin brother, Apollo. To this day, Pegasus hasn't figure out what drew him to the goddess in the first place. They were nothing alike. He was solid ground, and she was fire.

"You need to pull yourself together. I've come with grave news from the Underworld."

"Pff. What's Hades plotting this time?"

"It has nothing to do with Hades."

She takes a large sip from the bottle, sloshing liquid on her now stained white gown. She wipes her wet lips with the back of her forearm, reminding Pegasus of the lowly mortal soldiers he's had to assist once or twice in his lifetime.

"Out with it already, boy. Your presence is killing my buzz."

With a deep breath, he continues. "The Furies have escaped."

Artemis raises her eyebrows a fraction. The gesture is fleeting, and soon her attention returns to her drink.

"Did you hear what I said?" Pegasus presses.

"Yeah, I heard you. I don't know why you think I should care about the Furies."

In a rare show of impatience, he rubs his face, then fixates his stare on a potted plant hanging from the pergola.

"May I remind you that you were the reason the Furies were imprisoned in the Underworld in the first place? And also that they vowed to seek revenge once they escaped?"

Artemis tsks. "If you're concerned about my well-being, you shouldn't be, my dear. I'm a goddess. The Furies can't harm me."

"No, but they can hurt your wolves now that they're living in the human realm."

A flash of anger shines in her eyes as she straightens her back. He's relieved to see a proper reaction from her—only his relief came too soon.

"They've chosen to become mortals. If the Furies come for them, I don't give a damn. Let their mate defend the fools. She's so special, after all."

"Just because she bears your mark doesn't mean she'll be able to stop the Furies. She's no match for them." Pegasus raises his voice, not believing that Artemis would let her wolves be harmed.

She pushes the bottle of whiskey aside and staggers to her feet. "That's too fucking bad. Now, if you only came here to deliver that news, you can leave."

"Your wolves' mate is pregnant," Pegasus finally reveals. He didn't want to part with that information, afraid Artemis would do something to harm the woman in a fit of jealousy.

As he expected, that news has the most significant impact on the goddess. Her bright green eyes, which were flashing anger a minute ago, are swimming with absolute pain now. He almost feels sorry for her.

She turns her back to him, her shoulders sagging forward. Pegasus is overwhelmed with the need to touch her, offer comfort. But he knows better than to approach her when she's wounded like that—or at any time, for that matter.

"Are you certain?" she asks in a small voice.

"Yes."

She doesn't speak for a minute, and with each passing second, Pegasus feels the atmosphere become tenser. Finally the goddess whirls around, her loose, almost see-through dress billowing with the movement.

But only her garment is as light as air. Artemis's expression is the complete opposite. Storm clouds seem to gather in her gaze, and her face resembles the marble statues erected in her honor.

"I hope the Furies have something extra wicked planned for them, then."

Pegasus's stomach clenches as he watches the goddess he once held on a pedestal become a monster. "You don't mean that."

"Oh yes, I do."

## 1

RED

"Are you ready?" the technician asks with a twitch of her lips.

"Hell yeah," Sam answers enthusiastically, even though the woman wasn't looking at him.

Serena, another supernatural who works at Crimson Hollow Hospital, smiles broadly. She has fae blood, but no one knows how close her connection to the fairer folk really is.

"I'm more than ready," I reply.

Tristan laces his fingers with mine. I look up, meeting his gaze, and as usual, my heart does a backflip. We've been mated for a little over seven months now, and I can't believe I get to call him, Dante, and Sam mine. Sometimes I think I'm dreaming.

Serena squirts cold gel on my huge twenty-eight-weeks belly and uses the transducer probe to spread the slimy texture over my lower abdomen. We found out that I'm carrying triplets the first time we came here, but today we finally caved and decided to learn the babies' genders.

At first, I didn't want to know, but last month, Dante had a vision about them, and Tristan and Sam thought it was unfair that he knows more about our babies than we do.

"All right, here they are," Serena says, pointing at the moving black-and-white blur on the screen.

I squint, trying to make out their individual shapes. Serena applies gentle pressure on my belly as she glides the probe, which squeezes my full bladder.

"Whoa, I see the pee-pee of one. It's a boy!" Sam points at the monitor.

"Actually, that's the arm." Serena chuckles. "But you're not wrong. This one is a boy."

Sam tackles Tristan, hugging him sideways. "One for our team!"

Grumbling, Tristan replies, "Take it easy."

I glance quickly at Tristan and catch his upturned lips. He might not express his feelings as loudly as Sam, but he's just as excited.

"You're silly. There's no team," I reply.

"Yes there is. Team Red." Dante winks at me, making me blush.

"Are you ready to know the gender of your second baby?" Serena asks.

"Yes!" Sam answers loudly enough that it counts for all of us.

"Congratulations, it's another boy."

"If you yell, I'm kicking you out," I warn Sam, who already had his arms raised for a celebration.

I turn my attention to the monitor, but from the corner of my eye, I see him and Tristan high-fiving each other. Silly men.

Serena frowns as she slides that probe left and right. "Hmm, I can't quite get a visual of the third baby's genitals. He or she is hiding from us."

"A hundred bucks it's another boy," Sam pipes in.

I grunt. "Oh God. I hope not. I can't handle another penis in the house." Tristan snorts while Serena raises an eyebrow at me.

"What? You don't think I have enough with this trio?" I point at the guys.

"I hear ya. In any case, it doesn't seem like we're finding out the gender of the third baby today."

I pout, sadder about that than I should be. Damn stupid hormones.

Serena hands me a tissue so I can clean myself, and then I slide off the bed and run to the bathroom. When I walk out, the guys have all the printouts from today's scan.

Dante steps closer and throws his arm around my shoulders. Leaning close to my ear, he whispers, "Don't worry, my love. It's not another boy. It's a girl."

"Really?" I squeak.

With a smile, he nods. "A beautiful blonde little girl, just like her mother." He tucks a strand of hair behind my ear, and then he caresses my cheek. The simple gesture gets me all choked up. Tears form in my eyes, and I'm two seconds away from bawling.

"Yo, what's going here?" Sam asks.

"You lost your bet." I wipe away the couple of tears that escaped.

"Huh?"

"Third baby is a girl," Dante replies.

"If you knew the genders already, why didn't you tell us?" Tristan asks.

"I didn't know. I only saw the girl clearly in my vision."

As if in response, I feel a kick, and instinctively I know it's my baby girl.

She's going to be a fighter, just like me.

<hr>

"I'm so excited for you, Red. And obviously I expect to be the godmother of one of your puppies," Kenya says.

"Of course you are. So, how are things with your mother?" I

take a big sip of my strawberry milkshake, one of my new cravings.

She sighs, sagging her shoulders forward and focusing on her fries. "Strained. She still hasn't really explained why she never told me about the supe community. I mean, she's still maintaining the same old excuse that she was trying to protect me, yada, yada, yada. But is that all?"

"Why would you think there's more?"

"Because. She gets super tense every time I bring up the subject. And when I ask about my father?" Kenya whistles. "Mom gets stiffer than a board. Total avoidance mode."

"I'm sure she'll come around eventually."

She pops a fry in her mouth, her eyes going out of focus as she chews. "I'm thinking about trying Zeke again."

"How many times have you tried?"

"Ten." She shrugs. "But who's counting? I don't get it. I've tried bargaining, pleading, but nothing will make him spill the beans. I thought imps lived for deals."

"Just please don't offer something you'll regret. He might be our ally, but he's still an agent of Hell."

Kenya squints, scrunching her nose. "I know, okay? I'm not about to sell my soul to him. Too bad Nina is out of town. I heard she's good in the acquiring intel department."

I sag against my seat. Nina skipped town soon after we defeated Harkon, and Billy has been a mopey mess ever since. I thought he would get over his crush on Leo's sister, but it turns out I was very wrong. Pair him with Nadine—who has every reason to not be Miss Sunshine—and we have Daria and Jane from the *Daria* cartoon on our hands. I'd get "Woe Is Me" T-shirts for both of them if I were meaner.

"Maybe I can talk to your mother. You know, use my huge pregnancy belly to gain sympathy points. I can even cry on demand. Anything will trigger the waterworks these days." I offer Kenya a smile. I'm glad that despite everything—aka me turning into a wolf shifter—we're still best friends.

"Thanks, I might take you up on your offer. So, who was the lucky winner on the daddy lottery?"

I rest my head in my hands. "Ugh. Sam. Can you believe it?"

In true Kenya fashion, she throws her head back and laughs. "That's priceless. I can't believe Sam will get to play the baby daddy for your folks."

"I know, right? Tristan or Dante would have been much better choices. I can already picture my mother's disapproving glance when she finally learns I got knocked up by the lead singer of a rock band. It was hard enough telling them I was pregnant and being vague about the father's identity."

"No shit. I know how my mother would react. Castration comes to mind." She snorts.

"If she only knew." I laugh.

"Bitch." Kenya throws a fry at me.

"Jokes aside, I can't tell my parents that I'm a wolf shifter mated to three alphas. My father knows about the supernatural community, but Mom is clueless."

"Tell me when your folks get here. I'll be there for moral support." Her eyes twinkle with mirth.

"Yeah, moral support, my ass."

Her gaze moves to a point over my shoulder, and her eyes widen as her jaw drops.

I know that look. She spotted someone she likes.

"Hubba hubba. Where did that piece of Heaven come from?"

I start to turn, but she grips my hand. "Don't look back yet. He's coming this way."

The guy in question walks by our table and takes a seat on the high stool in front of the counter. Immediately I see why Kenya was drooling all over her fries. The dude is definitely attractive, with long, tousled blond hair that reaches his shoulders and a physique designed to impress the ladies. He's talking to the waitress, so I can only see his profile, but even that's enough.

"He looks like he just stepped off a California beach." I drink from my milkshake to disguise that I'm ogling the stranger.

"Exactly, a Californian dreamboat." Kenya sighs.

In that exact moment, the stranger turns and looks straight at me. Shit. He totally caught me staring.

I should look down, but there's something in his eyes that hits me straight in the chest. Suddenly, I can't draw air in, and I start to panic.

"Red, what's wrong?" Kenya touches my arm.

Finally, I'm able to break away from the guy's creepy gaze and look at my friend.

"I don't know."

"Your face went white all of a sudden."

"I'm not feeling well. Can we go?"

"Yeah, sure."

I turn to where the stranger was sitting to see what he's doing, but he's gone.

## 2

---

### RED

I CAN'T SHAKE THE STRANGE FEELING THAT TOOK HOLD OF ME IN the diner. It's been a few hours since Kenya dropped me off at the compound, but my chest still feels heavy. That stranger who came into the diner is the cause for my current mood. If Kenya hadn't seen him too, I might have thought he was a figment of my imagination. But he was there, of that I'm sure. Only he didn't stay long enough for me scrutinize him further.

I'm in the Alpha Manor's kitchen, cooking dinner and attempting to forget what happened. I definitely don't want to mention the mysterious man to my mates. The last seven months have been blissfully stress free—at least where demons trying to kill everyone are concerned—and I don't want to worry them over a bad feeling that could be only a figment of my imagination. But maybe I should mention the guy to Dr. Mervina just to be safe.

Nadine comes through the door, bringing with her a flurry of snow, followed by Billy. But whereas Nadine is bundled up from head to toe, Billy is only wearing a leather jacket that does nothing to protect him from the unmerciful cold outside. He shakes his head, sending snow all over the floor.

"Hey, you'd better clean that up before it turns into mud," I warn. "I just cleaned the floor."

"Sorry, Red."

He goes in search of a mop while Nadine retraces her steps and wipes her boots on the rug outside. Not that it'll do any good, but points for trying. She removes her coat, draping it over a chair, and then proceeds to check what I'm cooking on the stove.

"It's Bolognese sauce. The babies are in the mood for some Italian."

Nadine signals fast with her hands, saying she's starved. It took me a while to learn sign language, but I was determined to master it so I could communicate with her while in human form. I can only talk to her telepathically when I'm a wolf, and since it's not safe for me to shift during the pregnancy, sign language is the only way we can connect.

Billy comes closer, eyeing the pan I'm cooking in, and asks, "I know you're eating for four, but damn, girl. That's a lot of sauce."

"First, I'm not a *girl*. Second, we're expecting company tonight."

"Who?"

"Jared, Armand, Leo, and—"

"Oh, Leo is coming?" Billy's voice sounds hopeful. No doubt he's planning to grill the guy about his sister, Nina. I can't believe Billy hasn't forgotten the fox spy after all this time.

"That's what I said. Oh, and Xander is coming too."

Nadine freezes on the spot, her eyes turning as round as saucers. She always reacts funny every time the bear alpha is mentioned, igniting my protective instincts. Xander wasn't the friendliest of people toward Nadine in the beginning. He's better now, but I can't put down my shield around him when it concerns her. She's part of my family now, just like Billy is.

"Shouldn't he be hibernating?" Billy asks.

"His sleuth is, but Xander isn't completely at ease yet, so he decided to sit this hibernation season out."

"Hello, anyone home?" Xander's booming voice sounds from the entryway, almost as if we'd summoned him by speaking his name.

"We're in the kitchen," I answer.

Nadine glances at the door she just used to come in, then at the one connecting the kitchen to the living room. Her deer-caught-in-headlights gaze clues me in that she's considering running out into the cold again.

Xander comes into the kitchen, making the room seem half its size. Tall with broad shoulders and a wild mane that matches his personality, he's a sight to behold and fear. But that didn't stop me from challenging the bear shifter last year when he attacked Tristan.

"Hi, Xander. You're early," I say.

"You have no idea how difficult it is for me to step outside in this weather."

I raise an eyebrow at him. Bear shifters usually keep to themselves, and it shows. He has the social skills of a spoon.

"Ah, sorry. Hi, Red. How are you?" he adds.

"I'm fine. Thanks for asking." I smirk at him.

His gaze moves to Nadine, who is now standing in a corner, trying to appear smaller. "Hey, kid. What are you doing there? I'm not going to hurt you."

Her expression turns into a glare. She signals with her hands, fast and furious, before she stomps out of the kitchen.

"What was that?" Xander asks.

"She said she's not a kid, and the last part was 'bite me, asshole,'" Billy replies with amusement.

"Maybe you ought to teach that kid some manners, Red. Jeez."

I scoff. "Like she said, she's not a kid. But maybe you're the one who needs to curb your wild nature a bit."

"I'm a shifter! How am I supposed to do that?"

"What's going on? Ah, I see Xander is here." Dante walks into the kitchen, veering to my side to kiss me on the cheek. "Is he misbehaving already?"

Squinting, I glance at the bear alpha. "Only a little."

"I was not." He takes his leather jacket off in a jerky manner.

"He already managed to piss off Nadine." Billy chuckles.

"You have a big mouth, kid," Xander grumbles and takes a seat by the table.

"Who has a big mouth?" Sam comes in through the kitchen door, letting cool air and snow in. He's followed by his bandmates: Jared, Armand, and Leo—aka the druid, the vamp, and the fox. Man, that sounds like the start of a bad joke.

"Hey! I just mopped the floor." Billy glares at the foursome.

"Oh, look at that, honey. You've successfully domesticated the pup." Sam laughs.

"I'm not a pup. I'm nineteen!"

"Sam," I say in a chastening tone.

"It's not my fault he can't handle the truth." He shrugs.

"I'm only two years younger than Red. If I'm a pup, so is she, which means you're a perv."

Jared and Armand whistle while Sam's easygoing expression turns murderous. "What did you say, Billy?" He takes a step toward the former omega, a position the pack no longer has.

No doubt sensing the change in Sam's demeanor—who is now projecting his alpha dominance to the max—Billy's face blanches.

"Never mind. Call me when diner is ready." Faster than lightning, he swirls around and bolts from the kitchen.

"What a brat." Sam glowers at the door for a second before turning to me. "Our kids won't be like that." He kisses me on the lips before I can reply.

"Like what?" Tristan asks from the kitchen's entrance. "And

what happened to Billy? He took off like the devil was after him."

"He ran his mouth," Xander replies.

Tristan rolls his eyes. "What's new?"

"It's all your fault for being too easy on him." Sam crosses his arms.

"I'm not too easy on him." Tristan walks across the kitchen and not too gently pushes Sam out of the way so he can hug me from behind. "How was your day, my love?"

"Good. I had lunch with Kenya."

Mentioning my lunch date with her brings the blond stranger to the forefront of my mind. I tense without meaning to.

"What's wrong?" Tristan asks.

"Nothing. I'm a bit tired."

"Step away from the stove immediately and let us finish prepping dinner." Tristan takes the wooden spoon from my hand and passes it on to Dante before he steers me to a chair.

"I can finish cooking," I protest, but it's half-hearted. I'm glad to be off my swollen feet.

At once, all the guys start buzzing about in the kitchen, even our guests. I lean back in my chair and watch as seven powerful supernatural creatures work in synchronized harmony.

A warm and fuzzy feeling spreads through my chest. I smile and place my hands on my belly.

"See, little ones? This is what love is all about."

---

AFTER DINNER, I LET THE GUYS TAKE CARE OF THE CLEANUP WHILE I head for the babies' nursery. I'm staring at nothing in particular, thinking about the man from the diner again, when Sam walks in carrying a huge box.

"Hello, my love. We got a package from your folks."

"Another one?" I smile, but it's not completely genuine.

He sets the box down. "This is one of three." He looks at me and frowns. "What's wrong?"

Darn it. I can't really hide anything from my mates.

"It's nothing." I drop my gaze to the box.

Sam approaches and holds me by the shoulders. "Red? You know you can tell me anything, right?"

I lift my chin to meet his gaze. "I'm fine."

"You're sad."

"It's probably pregnancy blues," I say, even though I know it's not that.

Sam caresses my cheek with the tips of his fingers. "I know a way I can make you feel better." He beams, showing off the dimples I adore.

Desire immediately curls around the base of my spine and spreads throughout my body. My libido increased tenfold when I became a wolf shifter, but it's tripled now that I'm pregnant.

"Oh yeah? How?" I smile lazily, my gaze dropping to his mouth.

Sam slides his fingers to the back of my head, grabbing a chunk of hair in the process, and forces me to look into his eyes again. "I have several ideas, but we can start with this." He lowers his mouth to mine, searing my lips with a panties-dropping kiss.

I'd melt completely into his arms if it weren't for my huge belly in the way. Sam's tongue is incendiary, even when he's taking things slowly. I throw my arms around his neck, needing to be as close to him as possible.

A throat clearing brings a premature ending to our kiss. Tristan and Dante are now standing near the door, each carrying a similar box to the one Sam brought in.

"I suppose they sent one for each baby," Dante says by way of explanation. He sets the box down and, using his sharp fingernail, cuts the packaging tape. He then pulls a large object from within, which was buried under little pieces of packaging foam.

"Oh my God." I cover my mouth with my hands.

Dante, Tristan, and Sam are all staring at the white wolf rocker my parents sent me.

After a moment, Dante turns to me. "Are you sure your parents don't know you're a wolf shifter?"

"Of course not. Mom doesn't even know that supernatural creatures exist."

"Do you think the other rockers are all the same?"

"If they're all wolves, I'll say we have a traitor in the midst," Tristan replies with a smirk.

It takes less than a minute to unveil that, indeed, my parents sent wolf rockers to all babies. It would have been hard to pinpoint who gave them the suggestion if it weren't for the wolf with the pink bow. Only Dante knew I was expecting a girl.

"It was you!" I point accusatorily at him.

"Me what?" His eyes are widely innocent, but the corners of his lips twitch up.

"Wait, Dante told your parents to send wolf rockers?" Sam looks at us. "How do you know?"

"The bow." Tristan chuckles.

Dante gives up his attempt to hide his smirk and lets a full smile blossom on his handsome face. I shake my head, trying to downplay the effect his expression has on me. The sense of doom I was feeling only a moment ago is gone. In its place, the most immense feeling of peace and love has taken over.

Out of the blue, I begin to cry.

Dante's smile wilts to nothing. "Red? What's wrong?"

I wipe away the fat tears that are rolling down my cheeks. "I'm not sad, I promise. These are happy tears."

Immediately, my mates form a cocoon around me, hugging me from all sides. Their warmth washes over me, making me feel like I'm the most cherished woman on the planet. I feel our babies move, almost as if they can sense their dads' love too.

"We're happy too, my love. Beyond happy," Tristan says.

"I know," I reply.

"I think maybe we should head for bed." Sam places a kiss on my shoulder.

"I agree. I'm feeling bone-tired all of a sudden." Dante runs his hand down my arm, sending a shiver down my back.

"Let's go, then," Tristan replies tightly.

My nipples become as hard as pebbles, and heat pools between my legs. I know exactly what we'll be doing in bed, and I'm already shaking with anticipation. "Sleeping sounds absolutely divine."

3

RED

I WAKE UP WITH A START. MY HEART IS POUNDING AGAINST MY RIB cage, wrapped in a sense of anxiety and fear. I reach for the lamp's switch. With a click, a soft orange glow spreads throughout my room, but even the light can't make me feel less agitated. I try to throw my legs to the side of the bed, but something bulky on my middle prevents me. I glance down, meeting a mountain instead of my flat belly.

*What the hell!*

With a hard yank, I push the sheet aside. It takes me a few seconds for my sluggish brain to comprehend what I'm seeing. When it finally does, I yell.

"Oh my God. Oh my God. What's this?" I roll my large T-shirt up, revealing a round and tight belly.

The main lights to the room turn on, and Grandma is standing by the door with Elliot at her heels. "Amelia, what's wrong?"

I'm frozen, unable to speak as I glance at the bizarre pregnant belly I didn't have yesterday.

"Grandma, please tell me this is a nightmare."

Her eyes round as she focuses on my midsection. "Oh my."

"'Oh my'? Is that all you have to say?"

She walks in and stops by the side of the bed. "I don't know what you want to hear, hon."

"Is this some kind of practical joke? This belly can't be real, right?" I poke my side, and holy shit, I feel a kick. I gasp. "There's something alive inside of me."

Grandma flattens her palm over my belly, furrowing her eyebrows. Then she looks at me. "What do you remember about yesterday? Did you do or see anything strange?"

"No. Grandma, you're scaring me."

Without a word, she walks out.

"Where are you going?" I get up fast and almost end up falling forward. Damn, this stupid belly weighs a ton. Also, I have to pee. Badly.

I make a beeline to the bathroom and relieve myself, then peer at my reflection in the mirror. With shaking hands, I lift my T-shirt again. I look like I'm about to pop. And honestly, I do feel something pressing against my rib cage. I check my boobs as well, and holy fuck, what happened to my nipples? They're twice the size they used to be and three shades darker.

*No.* Shaking my head, I walk backward. *This must be some crazy nightmare.*

When I return to my room, Grandma is back, carrying a book and a branch of burning sage.

"What are you doing?"

"Shh, child. I'm trying to concentrate."

Several questions are on the tip of my tongue, but I wait. She begins to mumble words in a strange language and walk around me, swishing the burning sage from side to side. The smoke stings my nose and gives me a fit of sneezes.

After ten minutes of crazy mumbo jumbo, Grandma stops and closes the book in her hand with a loud thud.

"A spell has been cast," she announces like it's the most natural thing in the world.

"Uh, a what?"

"No time to explain. Get dressed. We need to visit some friends of mine. The magic is too strong for me to undo it by myself."

*Okay, I'm definitely having a nightmare. But then why the hell am I not waking up?*

Since I'm stuck here, I do as Grandma told me. But to my dismay, I don't own any clothes that fit. The T-shirt I'm wearing now barely does, and only because it's three times larger than my regular size. I keep it on and force myself into a pair of leggings. My ass is also much bigger than it used to be. I hope I don't bust a seam.

On my way out, I grab my cell phone. If by some bizarre occurrence this isn't a dream, I need to be able to reach Kenya. Grandma is ready to go when I join her in the living room. The clock mounted on the wall shows it's only thirty minutes after midnight. I glance at the phone screen. It's Friday, so Kenya must be out. The question is, why am I not with her?

Elliot barks and wags his tail, thinking we're going on a field trip.

Grandma turns to him. "I'm sorry, buddy. You can't come with us."

She heads out into the freezing January weather, but one glimpse at my coat hanging from the peg makes my heart sink. No chance in hell I'll fit that.

"Are you coming or not, Amelia?"

*Shit. What happened to my sweet grandma?*

This must be a nightmare. She's acting like she doesn't care that her granddaughter woke suddenly pregnant in the middle of the night.

I put the coat on, leaving it unbuttoned, then wrap myself with the thickest woolen scarf I own.

The moment I step foot into the ice-cold weather, my bladder complains. I gotta pee again. *Are you freaking kidding me? I turn around.*

"Where are you going?" Grandma asks.

"I'll be right back."

---

"WHERE ARE WE GOING?" I BRACE AGAINST THE DOOR WHEN THE road becomes rough.

"I already told you, child. We're going to see some of my friends."

"Grandma, are you a witch?" I ask.

She doesn't answer right away. We hit a pothole in the road, and I feel it all the way up my spine. I also sense a kick, which only serves to freak me out more.

"Grandma?" I press.

"Yes, Amelia. I'm a witch."

*Okay, deep breaths, Red. Deep breaths.* "Am I a witch too?"

She glimpses quickly at me. "Possibly."

Blinking fast, I stare at the dark road ahead. I wait for another freak-out moment, and when it doesn't come, I know the reason. I'm most certainly dreaming. I must be in deep slumber since there's no signs I'm going to wake up any time soon, so I might as well feed my imagination.

"Okay. Cool."

"Cool?" Grandma replies.

I shrug. "What do you want me to say?"

"Many things. I certainly didn't expect you to be so blasé about it."

"Does Dad know?"

"Yes."

"Is he a witch too?"

"No. Our power can only be transferred to female born."

We arrive at the sad-looking shack in the woods. It kind of reminds me of Grandma's house, only this one is covered in twisty vines, granting it a freaky appearance. The car's headlights aren't helping the case much either.

Grandma kills the engine and the lights and slides out. I follow suit, wrapping my body to try to keep warm. The front door of the shack opens, and out come four women dressed in dark cloaks. I can't see their faces, but I can sense the strange energy surrounding them.

I wait by the car while Grandma strides forward to meet them. She speaks in hushed tones and then glances over her shoulder. Her friends turn to look at me as well, and on instinct, I cover my belly with my hands. Shit. I've been pregnant for less than an hour and I'm already protective of my baby.

"Come, Amelia." Grandma waves me over.

Reluctantly, I move forward. It snowed recently, and the snow crunches under my boots.

"Don't be afraid, child." The tallest of the women pushes her hood back, revealing a long jet-black mane and a face as white as the ground.

"I'm not afraid."

"Because you think you're dreaming," she replies calmly.

I widen my eyes. "I don't think. I *know*."

The woman drops her eyes to my protruding belly. "Three babies, each one fathered by a different… *wolf*."

"What?" I squeak.

"What does that mean, Veronica?" Grandma asks, looking at me in a funny way now.

I cross my arms. "Exactly. What kind of disturbing dream is this?"

Focusing on my ire is easier than dwelling on the way I'm dreaming about being knocked up by wolves. Shit. I don't even like channels like National Geographic, unless it's Shark Week. I mean, how can I not like Shark Week? I suppose I should be glad that I'm not pregnant by three sharks.

I shake my head. Fuck. Even in my dreams I have rambling thoughts.

"I don't know. But I also sense a great spell has been cast all over town, and it seems to be linked to your granddaughter."

"That's just great," I mumble.

"We must form a circle," another one of Grandma's friends says.

"A spell strong enough to affect the entire town might be beyond our ability to break with a circle," a third woman chimes in.

"We can always call Geor—" Veronica starts.

"No. Absolutely not. We're not going to her. There's a reason we formed this coven," Grandma replies sharply.

Veronica looks at the starless sky. "The longer we wait, the harder it will be to undo the magic. We must act fast."

She walks toward the forest, and her companions follow her. They disappear around the shack, but I don't move from my spot. Grandma offers me her hand. "Come on, Amelia. Let's find out what's going on."

I reach for her, but before we touch, everything goes dark. Then I have the feeling that I'm inside a vortex. I'm spinning out of control, but somehow I can't scream or see anything.

As sudden as the whirling motion came, it vanishes. When my vision returns, Grandma is gone, and I'm no longer in a forest in front of a spooky shack. I'm now in the middle of Crimson Hollow's square, about to have a heart attack.

Fuck. As dreams go, this is one is seriously messed up. I'm done suffering it alone. I pull my cell phone from my pocket to call Kenya.

She answers on the first ring. "Red, you're not goi—"

"Kenya, you need to help me. I don't know what's going on. I woke up in the middle of the night with the biggest pregnant belly known to man, and I don't know how that happened."

"Whoa, slow down," she replies.

"I can't slow down. I know this must be a freaking dream, but I'm not waking up."

"Riiight. You guys are super hilarious. Who else is involved in this?"

"This is not a joke, damn it! I'm freaking out." I begin to pace while ripping at my hair.

"I gotta give it to you, Red. That's a pretty impressive acting job. But I'm not falling for it. I'll see you tomorrow, crazy girl," Kenya says before she ends the call.

I stare at my phone. *I can't believe this. She hung up on me!*

An icy gust of wind comes from my left, chilling me to the bone and reminding me that I'm not wearing much. Dream or no dream, I have to get out of here. I glance around, but everything is closed besides the Five-Headed Dragon music venue. The smart thing would be to go in, but I can't be seen looking like this.

*If this is only a dream, what does it matter?*

"Ah damn it," I mutter and head toward the busy establishment.

Two steps forward and I feel an eerie sensation at the back of my neck. I turn around and find a tall man with long blond hair in full armor where a second ago no one stood. But what catches my attention the most is the strange glint in his eyes. It seems like they're glowing. I'm leery of him in an instant.

"Who are you?" I ask, taking a step back.

"Don't be afraid, Red."

My legs tense, ready to bolt. "How do you know my name?"

He glances over his shoulder in a cagey manner. "We don't have much time. You have to come with me."

"Hell to the no. I'm not going anywhere with you."

This is it. I have to flee. *Come on legs, move.*

He takes a step forward. "The fear you're feeling isn't real. I swear I'm here to help."

He reaches for me, and I do the only thing I'm capable of since my legs are frozen.

I scream.

## 4

## SAMUEL

"The usual, Sam?" Donny, one of the bartenders at Five-Headed Dragon, asks.

I answer with a nod while I scan the crowd to get a feel of the assortment tonight. Crimson Hollow is small, and most likely I've already slept with most of the bangable chicks here, but there's always the random hot out-of-towner dying for a taste of small-town life.

I see two girls in particular who haven't stopped gawking. They were also in front of the stage during the first half of our set, undressing me with their hungry eyes. Maybe tonight will be a double treat.

Leo stops next to me and follows my line of sight. "I see you've found your mark already."

"Sure have." Without breaking eye contact with the girls, I take a sip of my beer. Then I smile, showing my famous dimples, a sure thing to get me laid.

Predictably, they giggle and avert their gazes, only to look at me again from under their eyelashes.

That's my cue. I turn to Donny. "Two more beers, please."

Like a pro, he slides the cold bottles across the bar toward my waiting hands.

"Wish me luck," I say to Leo.

"Like you need it," he grumbles.

Shit, *he* needs to get laid.

With alcoholic beverages in hand, I veer toward my marks. They're all fake coy smiles when I stop in front of their high-top table. They're acting like all girls who come to see the band, but tonight, their predictable behavior is turning me off. I push the strange notion aside.

"Good evening, ladies. Did you enjoy the first half of the show?"

"Oh yeah. We loved it," the short brunette with fake tits replies.

"We came all the way from San Diego just to see you play," her companion, a red-head with freckles, adds.

"You don't say?"

"Oh yeah. We've watched, like, all of your videos online a million times." She laughs a little too loudly, and it takes great effort not to wince.

"Drinks?" I offer them the beers I got.

"Sure." The brunette reaches for the bottles.

I'm about to ask for their names when a female voice says from behind me, "Samuel Wolfe, you'd better have a damn good explanation for why you're flirting with those two bimbos instead of being home with Red."

"What is she talking about? Who's Red?" one of the girls asks, but I'm no longer paying attention to them.

I turn, coming face-to-face with Kenya Arantes, Sheriff Arantes's daughter. She's a regular at our concerts and one of the few attractive local girls I haven't fucked. Not because she blew me off but because she's the sheriff's daughter, and I don't wanna risk castration. When I hit puberty and started to notice girls, I made a concerted effort to put Kenya firmly in the friend zone. So despite the fact that she's a ten and a firecracker—usually a dangerous combination to me—I never had any desire to hook up with her.

"Kenya, fancy seeing you here." I smile. Maybe this is all a ploy to get my attention.

"Cut the crap, Sam. What the hell are you doing here? I thought the band was in hiatus."

"Is this lunatic bothering you, Samuel?" one of the girls asks.

Kenya narrows her eyes to slits and walks around me. "Listen up, bitches. You'd better pack your pathetic skank asses and hit the road. Don't make me show you how I treat Pornhub rejects who flirt with my best friend's husband."

The girls look at me with wide eyes. "You're married?" they shriek at the same time.

I lift my hands. "Whoa, I'm not married." Now Kenya is pissing me off. "What the hell? What's the matter with you?"

She drops her jaw and looks at me like I've just grown a second head. "You're joking, right?"

"Excuse me? You're the one who's spewing crazy lies and I don't even know why. Are you on drugs?"

Kenya looks over my shoulder. "What the fuck are two still doing here? Get out!" She makes a fake charge toward the out-of-towners and they scramble. I don't blame them. She looks completely deranged.

"That's fucking it! I'm calling your mother." I pull my cell phone out.

"Ha ha. Okay, Sam. You can stop with the joke now. Did Red put you up to this?"

"For the love of God, who the fuck is Red?" I throw my hands up in the air.

"What's going on here?" Jared, the band's guitar player, stops next to me.

"Kenya decided today is the day for practical jokes. Only she doesn't know when to stop." I glower at her.

"What's the joke?" Jared asks.

"Apparently I'm married to some chick named Red," I reply, rolling my eyes.

"Who? Wait, doesn't Wendy Redford have a granddaughter that goes by that nickname?" Jared rubs his chin.

Kenya throws her hands out by her sides. "Fucking great. You're in on it too. You know what? Let's call her."

Her phone starts to ring at that precise moment. "I'll be damned. It's Red. It's like she knows you're up to no good, Samuel Wolfe."

"This ought to be good," I mumble.

"Red, you're not goi— Whoa, slow down." Kenya pauses, frowning, then turns to me with narrowed eyes. "Riiight. You guys are super hilarious. Who else is involved in this?"

I trade a glance with Jared, still completely clueless about what's going on. He shrugs.

A woman shrieks on the other side of the line, making Kenya pull the phone away from her ear with a grimace for a second. "I gotta give it to you, Red. That's a pretty impressive acting job. But I'm not falling for it. I'll see you tomorrow, crazy girl."

"So, your friend has no clue about me, right?" I ask with a smirk, then take a sip of my beer.

Squinting, Kenya replies, "So she says, but she's still very much knocked up, and *you* are the father. Well, at least one of the fathers."

I choke on my drink. "Excuse me?"

"Don't believe me? I'll show you." Kenya swipes her finger over her phone's screen until she finds what she's looking for. "Here, I took this two days ago."

She shoves her phone practically on my face, but I see nothing but her standing next to a blonde chick. A feel a strange tug, almost as if I should know her friend, but I definitely don't. I'd remember her for sure. She's just my type.

"What am I supposed to be seeing here?" I ask.

"Are you blind? It's Red, very much pregnant, you, and your brothers."

Jared moves closer and says, "No. It's just you and Red. She's not preggers."

Kenya moves the phone away from me and stares at the picture. "No. That's impossible." She begins to swipe the screen frantically. "What the fuck! They're all gone. How?"

Watching Kenya unravel in front of me over some fake pictures is starting to concern me. I don't think she's joking anymore. "Kenya, are you sure you didn't take anything? You're acting super strange."

"No, I didn't take anything." She lifts her gaze to meet mine. "But you're right about one thing. Something very strange is going on."

With phone glued to her ear, she begins to turn around. "Hey, where are you going?"

"To find answers."

She pushes her way through the throng of people, heading toward the exit.

"Shouldn't we follow her?" Jared asks.

"Yes" is on the tip of my tongue, but then I turn, my gaze colliding with an angel with white-blonde hair and a sinful mouth. Her eyes beguile me, and the urge to make sure Kenya is okay vanishes.

"Nah, she'll be fine. We have a set to finish. We can't disappoint our fans."

## 5

### RED

"GET AWAY FROM ME, YOU PERV!" I RETREAT, BUT I'M NOT USED to this huge belly, so I end up falling on my fat ass.

"Hey, leave her alone!" Kenya screams from somewhere nearby. She must have come from the music venue.

The stranger turns toward her and lifts his hands. "I'm not trying to harm her. Calm down."

"Calm down, my ass." Kenya stops in front of me with her cell phone out. "I'm calling the sheriff, asshole."

The guy looks into the distance and frowns. "We don't have much time. Your friend needs to come with me right now."

"How about I call her mates, buddy? Did you know Red is married to three big guys who can turn you into pudding?" Kenya takes a menacing step toward him.

*Wait, what?*

"You're not affected," he tells Kenya, sounding surprised.

I try to get up, but it's almost impossible with this big belly. Suddenly, someone lifts me from behind.

"There you go, Red," Zeke Rogers, the owner of Zeke's Sweet Treats, says. "What's going on here?" He stares at Kenya and then at the blond dude who is under her wrath.

"This guy tried to kidnap Red." Kenya points at the man, who's becoming transparent.

"Whoa, what's wrong with him?" I ask.

"Ah, shit. Are you a ghost?" Kenya moves closer to me.

He groans and then vanishes completely.

"Oh my God. What's happening?" I ask no one in particular.

Zeke approaches the place where the guy was standing two seconds ago. He crouches and picks up a handful of snow, bringing it to his nose. He curses after taking a whiff.

"What is it?" Kenya asks.

"Nothing good." He stands up again and looks at me. "What happened? And why are you underdressed like that?"

"I had nothing to wear." I pull the lapels of my jacket closer together.

"Come on, Red. Don't you think you're taking this prank too far?" Kenya puts her hands on her hips.

"I'm not pranking anyone. Why won't you believe me?" I grit out. "This is the worst dream ever. I want to wake up now."

From the corner of my eye, I catch Kenya and Zeke exchange a meaningful glance.

"What?" I ask.

Zeke squints, pinching his lips together. He opens his mouth to say something when suddenly his entire frame freezes. Slowly, he whirls around and sweeps the area. "Something isn't right."

A shiver runs down my spine, and the small hairs on the back of my neck stand on end. He can say that again.

"What do you sense?" Kenya asks.

"No time to explain. Let's go to my store. Quickly now." He grabs my arm and steers me across the square.

"What's going on?"

"Please, no questions until we're inside," he replies.

I glance at him, noticing how his facial expression is now twisted into a grimace.

"Zeke, are you okay?"

"Holy shit, man. Your eyes!" Kenya points out.

Angling my body so I can peer at his face properly, I see what she means. His eyes are glowing red. *What the fuck!* I try to break free from his hold, but he grips me tighter.

"Let go of me!" I struggle.

"Red, relax. It's Zeke. He won't harm you." Kenya looks at me as if I'm crazy.

Panic is making me all choked up. Out of nowhere I begin to cry. This is so stupid and so not me. I should be fighting or trying to run away. Instead, I'm a sobbing mess. What's wrong with me?

Before I know it, I'm inside Zeke's bakery. He finally drops my arm and proceeds to lock the door and shut the blinds.

Kenya grabs me by the shoulders and looks into my eyes. "Don't cry, Red. Everything will be all right."

"No it won't!" I push her off me. "I woke up with this huge belly, and I found out my grandmother is a witch. To top that off, a strange man tries to kidnap me, and Zeke is…." I glance at him. "I don't even know what he is."

"Red, this is very important. Where did you wake up?" he asks with a frown marring his forehead.

"In my bed."

"In the compound," Kenya adds.

"Compound? No, in my bedroom at Grandma's." Kenya and Zeke share another glance, pissing me off. "What's going on?"

"You don't remember Sam, Tristan, or Dante?" Kenya moves closer, and I don't like the glint of worry in her eyes one bit.

"The Wolfe triplets?"

"Yeah, your mates."

"My mates," I repeat like an idiot because I can't believe what my best friend is saying. "What's that even supposed to mean? Like roommates?"

Kenya narrows her eyes. "You're not pulling my leg, are you?"

"No! I swear to God, I have no idea what's going on."

"Okay. Okay. There's no need to panic. We'll figure this out." Zeke approaches me, but considering he's definitely not human, I step away.

"If she's afraid of you, then she really doesn't remember anything. And I bumped into Sam and Jared earlier and they had no idea who Red was."

"It seems that whatever spell was cast in Crimson Hollow, it wiped everyone's memories, but it didn't affect us," Zeke points out.

"Why not us?" Kenya asks, alarmed.

Zeke rubs his chin and begins to pace. "I don't know. But the guy who was trying to take Red somewhere was not from around here."

"What was he?" I ask, guessing by the way he simply vanished that he's not human either.

"A ghost, right?" Kenya turns to Zeke.

He shakes his head. "No, not a ghost. Something more powerful than that. A deity from Olympus."

"Shit. Do you think Artemis is behind this?"

I raise my arm. "Wait a second and back up. Artemis as in the goddess?"

"Oh, honey. You really don't remember a thing," Kenya says, her eyes full of pity.

"Don't look at me like that. If I'm not dreaming and I've truly lost my memories, how do I get them back? I was with Grandma not too long ago. She took me to meet some of her friends, and I'm guessing they were all witches."

"And what happened?" Zeke probes.

"Nothing. As soon as I got there, I was sent to the square."

"Were they planning on breaking the spell?" He continues to scrutinize me. It's unnerving.

"I think so."

"It's possible that whoever is responsible for this mess doesn't want you recovering your memories any time soon." He walks behind the counter and begins to collect random items, placing them on top.

"What are you going to do?" Kenya moves closer, eyeing the stuff Zeke placed there.

"I don't have all the answers, but I still have connections in Hell."

He sets a silver bowl on the counter and a dagger next to it.

"Are you going to perform some kind of satanic ritual?" My voice rises to a pitch while my heart drums away inside of my chest.

"Just a basic call to Downstairs. Nothing to be alarmed about."

Kenya retraces her steps to me and throws her arm around my shoulders. "Don't worry, Red. I won't let anything happen to you."

Zeke grabs the dagger and looks at us. "I'll need a small contribution from one of you."

"You want our blood?" I ask.

"Just a few drops."

"Why don't you use your own?" Kenya raises an eyebrow.

He gives us a droll look. "Because I'm an imp. My blood is tainted."

"Ugh. All right. You can have mine." She steps forward.

"Kenya, no. You could be inadvertently selling your soul."

"Okay, let's get this show running, because clueless Red is getting on my nerves." Zeke narrows his eyes.

"I'm sorry my memory loss is such a burden to you, asshole," I spit back.

"Red, don't antagonize the help," Kenya grits out.

"It's okay. I know she's not herself right now. All right, cookie. Give me your hand."

Kenya offers her palm to Zeke. He slides the dagger across, making her hiss. He then closes her hand, thus forcing the droplets of blood to fall into the silver bowl. She steps away while he tosses other ingredients in the bowl and begins to recite words in a strange language. He closes his eyes in concentration and his skin changes hue, turning grayish green. Freaky. How am I supposed to believe he's on our side when he looks like that?

He stops abruptly and stares at the bowl with a frown. "I don't understand. The spell isn't working."

"Don't tell us you need more blood." Kenya clutches her hand against her chest.

"No, what I got from you should have been enough." He lifts his chin to stare at my friend. "I know this isn't right the time to ask, but what are you?"

Kenya's spine turns rigid and her lips become nothing but a thin flat line. "*What* am I? You're joking, right? I'm fucking human, jackass."

Zeke opens his mouth to no doubt offer a retort but ends up clamping it shut.

I amble forward. "Maybe my blood will work."

He turns his blue eyes to me. "Are you sure?"

"Yes. If this is a nightmare, then there's no harm. And if it isn't, well, I have to do everything in my power to discover the culprit behind this chaos."

I offer him my hand, and without further ado, Zeke makes a cut. It hurts a little, though not as much as I thought it would. Once my blood is in the bowl, I walk backward until I'm standing next to Kenya.

"Now we can be called the slashed sisters," she jokes, but I don't sense any humor in her words. I don't know what's freaking her out the most, this situation or the fact that Zeke thinks she's not human.

The imp restarts the ritual. The moment the strange words

leave his mouth, the inside of the bowl begins to glow, bathing his face in crimson light. He peers inside, and once again his pupils change color to that freakish red.

"Damian, are you there?" he asks.

At least twenty seconds go by before I catch a disturbance in the glow from the bowl.

"Zeke, is that you?" a distorted voice replies.

"Yes, it's me."

"It's been a while. You haven't called in decades."

"I've been busy."

"I heard you made a trip to the Wastelands. That was reckless of you."

"It couldn't be avoided. Also, this call puts me in danger, so I'll cut straight to the point. Have you heard any whispers that the Olympian gods are back at their wicked games again?"

There's a pause in the communication, and I don't know if the connection is bad or Zeke's informant is thinking.

"Nothing concrete," the voice finally replies. "Just whispers of turmoil in Hades's domain. But you have to take that with a grain of salt. The Underworld isn't known for its stable and drama-free atmosphere."

"Is that all you know?"

"Yeah, sorry, man. I'd better go. I don't think I'm alone anymore."

The glow in the bowl vanishes. Zeke leans away and rubs his face.

"That's it?" I ask.

"Damn. It seems we donated blood for a whole lot of nothing." Kenya opens her hand to inspect the gash on her palm.

"I have one more person to call." Zeke pulls his cell phone out.

"Wait a minute. If you could call someone using modern technology, why didn't we try that first?" I ask.

"Because Trinity has been off the radar for months." I hear

the robotic voice of the voice mail lady, which brings forth a string of curses from Zeke. "See? I can't get a hold of her, which means we—"

Suddenly, the entire store begins to shake. I reach for the table nearby to avoid falling again. Kenya joins me there.

"What the hell is going on now?" she asks.

The front door bursts open, and the blond guy from before fills its frame. There's a big gash on his forehead now, and he looks pissed.

*Son of a bitch.*

6

———

RED

Kenya positions herself in front of me, getting into a defensive mode with her fists up. "If you want Red, you'll have to go through me, asshole."

The guy enters the bakery, shutting the door without touching it. Great. He has the ability to move shit with his mind.

Zeke walks around the counter with dagger in hand. "Stay back!" he warns.

The stranger looks at him and arches his eyebrows. "Put that weapon down, you fool. I'm not the enemy here."

"If you're not the enemy, who are you?" I ask.

"Wait a second. I remember you. You came into the diner yesterday," Kenya chimes in. "Only you didn't look like you just came from Comic Con."

I scramble for any memories of that meeting, but I come up empty.

The stranger glances at his ensemble and then at us again with a quizzical glint in his eyes. "I didn't come from Comic Con, wherever that place is. And yes, you saw me at the diner yesterday. I tried to stop them, but I wasn't strong enough."

40

"Stop who?" I press my hands on my belly, as if by doing so I'm shielding my baby from whatever harm is coming our way.

"The Furies," he answers.

"Aren't they some kind of mythological creatures?" Kenya glances at Zeke.

"Not creatures. They're the three goddesses of vengeance," the stranger answers. "Very dangerous and capricious. Artemis had them imprisoned in the Underworld many millennia ago, but they've escaped and are now thirsty for retribution."

"Son of a bitch," Zeke mutters. "Why would Artemis antagonize those three infernal goddesses?"

"They destroyed one of Artemis's sanctuaries on Earth, killing thousands of animals. To avoid a showdown between her and the mercurial trio, Hades agreed to imprison them."

"What does that have to do with me and Crimson Hollow?" I ask.

"They're after your mates." The stranger levels me with a hard stare.

That word again. *Mates.* My brain can't grasp the fact that I might be involved with three men at the same time. Out of everything I've seen and learned today, that's the most bizarre detail of all.

"Why would the Furies be after her mates?" Kenya asks.

"Because they were Artemis's wolves."

There's a pinch in my heart, a worry stemming from an unknown reason. I don't remember anything about my presumed mates, but the notion that they're in danger is giving me chest pain.

"Why can't the Furies take up their issues with Artemis? Why come here?" I ask in turn.

"As long as Artemis is in her Olympus sanctuary, they can't touch her. The Furies came for Samuel and Dante, who are easy prey now that they're living in the human realm," the man replies.

"Does she know?" I ask in a high-pitched voice, getting more nervous by the second.

He crosses his arms and stares at the floor. "I went to her first. She's not coming to aid."

I feel a kick and then pressure in my bladder. I have to pee again, but I can't go now. I need answers. "Why wouldn't she help them?"

Blondie lifts his chin to meet my gaze. "In Artemis's warped view, the moment they picked you over her, they died."

"That's just great." I throw my hands up in the air. "How do we fight three mean goddesses?"

"Oh, cookie. You don't fight the Furies. You stay the hell away from their path of destruction," Zeke interjects.

"The imp is right," the man says. "You can't fight the Furies."

"And you can?" Kenya raises an eyebrow.

He touches the gash on his forehead. "As you can see, no."

"They did that to you?" I cross my arms and my legs, because despite the horrible situation we're in, I still need to pee.

Zeke takes a step forward, narrowing his eyes. "You can't fight the Furies alone, so you're not a god. But you have access to Artemis, so that begs the question: Who are you?"

With a proud lift of his chin, he replies, "I'm Pegasus."

"Wait, like the winged horse from the legends?" Kenya looks the man up and down.

He turns to her, his expression solemn. "That's one of my forms."

I pull one of the chairs out and take a seat. I'm married to three guys, pregnant, Artemis hates my guts, and now her arch-enemies are set on destroying my world. That's just too much to handle.

"Red, are you okay?" Kenya touches my shoulder.

"No. I'm not okay." I turn to her. "We're standing in front of a mythical creature who just told us we have three vengeful goddesses gunning for us. And worst of all, I can't remember a thing."

"I can maybe help with that." Pegasus approaches me.

"How?" Kenya and I ask at the same time.

"I'm not a god, but I do have a bag of tricks at my disposal." He lifts his hand, stopping short of touching my forehead. "May I?"

I pull back, a knee-jerk reaction. "It depends. What are you going to do?"

"Try to undo what the Furies did."

"You have that power?" Kenya butts in.

"I don't know."

"Whoa. Hold on." I lift my hands. "I'm not sure if I want you messing with my head."

"I won't make it worse," he replies. "I promise."

Sucking my lower lip in, I glance at Kenya. She shrugs and says, "You have nothing to lose."

Taking a deep breath, I face Pegasus again. "Okay. Go ahead."

His touch is featherlight and warm. I sense a small vibration coming from his fingertips. It spreads across my forehead, leaving me light-headed for a moment. He pulls away, and three pair of expectant eyes are now trained on me.

"And? Did it work?" Kenya asks.

It takes me a moment to give her the answer. My heart sinks. "No. I still don't remember a thing."

Pegasus twists his face into a grimace while his eyes flash with guilt. "I'm sorry."

"You tried." I stand up. "But now I have to use the restroom."

I head for the back of the bakery. I do have to pee, but there's also another reason I want to be alone.

I'm already crying before I even lock the door. This is so frustrating. Feeling impotent and unhinged is so not me. I don't cry my eyes out in the face of problems; I face them head-on. God, being pregnant sucks.

When I return to the store, I walk into the middle of a heated discussion. Everyone shuts up when they see I've returned though.

"What?" I ask.

"We're debating what to do," Kenya replies

"And?"

"I want to take you to a safe place where the Furies can't harm you, but your friends are against the idea." Pegasus glares in Kenya and Zeke's direction.

"I'm not going anywhere. The Furies are after my mates, so there's only one course of action. I have to protect them."

"Have you not been listening to anything I said? You can't fight the Furies. You're only human."

I lift my chin. "I'm going to find my mates, and together we'll find a way to get rid of those bitches."

"That's what I'm talking about." Kenya moves to my side. "Besides, Red is more than just a human chick. She's the Mother of Wolves, sucker."

"I'm the what?"

Kenya waves her hand dismissively. "It doesn't matter. Now, let's go rescue your men."

"It's not safe out," Pegasus protests.

Zeke walks to the front window and peers through the blinds. "I don't see anyone outside, nor do I sense the presence of any god. If we're going after your mates, now's our chance."

Pegasus pinches the bridge of his nose and shakes his head. "This is a terrible idea. I'm telling you—"

"Enough stalling," I spit. "You don't know me, but I'm not one to just sit tight and wait for my problems to disappear."

"Sam is at Five-Headed Dragon. Let's get him and drive to the compound," Kenya says.

I square my shoulders, psyching myself up to officially meet one of my mates. I might be carrying his child, but in this fucked-up reality, he's a stranger. My stomach clenches in antic-ipation.

As if sensing where my head is, Kenya stops in front of me and begins to apply makeup to my face.

"Are you serious?" Zeke asks.

"Hey, they don't know each other, remember? I can't let my friend meet her mate with this just-out-of-bed style."

"Do I look that bad?" I ask.

"Oh no, honey. You can never look bad. But a little lipstick won't hurt."

A minute later she's done.

"Okay, let's do this," I say.

"Hold on, let me go out first." Pegasus veers for the door and sticks his head out. "The coast is clear for now."

He steps out first, looking like a veritable knight in shining armor. His uniform even has a crimson cape, for crying out loud.

Kenya and I follow him with our arms hooked together, and Zeke brings up the rear. We stride across the square as fast as we can, but I know I'm slowing the pace of the group with my humungous belly.

As we're about to cross the street in front of the music venue, the double doors open and a group of people walks out. Among them is Samuel Wolfe in the arms of a woman with long white-blonde hair. I don't remember being mated to him, but the pain that pierces my chest is real. And so is the red rage that clouds my vision.

I peel my lips back and snarl.

*That bitch is dead.*

## 7

## DANTE

My head is pounding, and my hold on the paintbrush is as unsteady as a giraffe on skates, but I can't quit now. The compulsion to paint is not unknown to me, but the inability to capture the image in my brain is. I dip the tip of the brush in the red paint and glide it on the canvas. It only takes a few strokes for me to know I'm going in the wrong direction. Again.

"Damn this to hell!" I hurl the brush into the distance, not caring where it lands. Pushing my long bangs back with one hand, I reach for the bottle of whiskey with the other.

The fiery amber liquid burns my throat as it goes down, and after a few gulps, I sway on the spot. With blurry vision, I look at my work in progress. More like a disgrace in progress. I got the general shape of a woman down, but it's the details of her face that are eluding me. Try as I might, I can't capture it on canvas. It's almost as if there's something blocking me.

I step away from the easel and amble toward my leather couch, plopping onto it and sloshing whiskey all over the front of my shirt. Whatever. It's already stained with oil paint, and when it's off my body, it's going straight to the trash bin.

Sinking against the back of the couch, I stare at the ceiling. I don't know what the hell is wrong with me. For the past three weeks, I've been trying to paint a woman with blonde hair and a red gown, but for the life of me, I can't finish it. Whenever I have visions, I can complete the art in a few hours. Only the compulsion to paint the mysterious woman isn't a vision, it's a raw need.

A couple of consecutive knocks on my front door echo in the room to disturb my peace, followed by Tristan's booming voice. "Dante! Open up."

"Fuck off!"

"You've been holed up in your studio for three weeks. Either you open the door or I'll tear it down."

"Fine. Tear it down," I dare, perversely wanting to see if Tristan will follow through with his threat this time.

A moment later, my door comes crashing down and Tristan appears in the frame, the personification of a wrathful god.

"There. Door down. Now you can't hide here unbothered anymore."

"Fucker." I take another large sip of my drink.

Tristan walks in, scrunching his nose. "Phew. It reeks in here. What the hell, Dante?"

"Bite me, Tristan."

"What's the matter with you? Mom has been worried sick. You haven't gone out or shifted the entire time you've been here. It's not healthy and you know it."

I glower at my brother, which he matches in intensity. Tristan takes the role of the older brother seriously, even if he's only older than me by a few minutes.

"Shit, you don't need to tell me. But I can't leave."

"You can't or you won't?" He raises an eyebrow.

I set the bottle of whiskey down on the floor and rest my elbows on my knees. "I can't. I've been trying to finish the portrait of that woman." Without looking up, I point at the canvas. "And until I do, I won't be able to do anything else."

"So, it's a vision thing?"

I lift my chin. "No, it's not a vision. It's… ah, shit. I can't explain. It's almost like a part of me is missing and it'll only be complete when I finish the painting."

Tristan turns toward the canvas. His eyebrows furrow and his jaw clenches hard. He doesn't speak for several beats as he stares at the unfinished painting. Then, out of the blue, he says, "I know her."

My spine goes rigid in an instant. "What do you mean?"

He shakes his head and glances at me. "I don't know. Just now, I got the strange sensation that I know the woman you're trying to capture. Only I have no clue where the notion is coming from. You didn't even finish her face."

I jump off the couch to stand next to him. "That's the problem. I can't get the details of her face right. It's almost as if there's a block in my head."

"And were you hoping hard liquor would help?"

I hear the criticism loud and clear.

"Don't fucking judge me, okay?"

"Well, drunk or not, you're coming with me."

"Have you not been listening to anything I said? I can't."

Tristan turns to me. "Are you saying you're physically unable to step foot outside?"

"Uh, I don't know."

"That's not a satisfactory answer. Sorry, brother."

"Sorry about what?"

"This."

Tristan's fist comes at me fast, too fast for me avoid. One hit and it's lights out for me.

## TRISTAN

"Was brute force necessary?" Mom asks as she peels Dante's eyelids open to check his pupils.

"Yes. He kept saying he couldn't leave. You know how Dante is with his idiosyncrasies."

"So you just punched him in the face?" She sets the flashlight aside and grabs a cloth to clean the blood from his nose, which is pointless to me.

"Just shove him under the shower. He's filthy." I cross my arms.

"I don't understand what's gotten into him. His gift never took him away from the real world for so long." She sets the cleaning rag aside and pushes his long bangs back.

"He claims it wasn't a vision."

She turns to me with eyebrows furrowed. "If not a vision, then what?"

"I don't know. But when you're done with him, you should go see the painting he's working on."

"Why?"

I look away, feeling embarrassed all of a sudden. I'm not prone to dwell on intuition and the other bullshit Mom and Dante are fond of. "It's a strange piece, and it moved me in a bizarre way."

"How so?" Mom probes.

I rub my face, trying to wash away the eerie déjà vu sensation that painting caused. "I don't know." Without looking in her direction again, I head for the door of the examination room. "I should go to bed. I have an early meeting tomorrow with Mayor Montgomery."

"Tristan, how many times do I have to tell you to not keep things bottled up?"

I glance over my shoulder. "I'm fine, Mom. Stop being so... motherly."

She rolls her eyes. "Yeah, yeah. I want to see how you'll fare when you have your own offspring to worry about."

A shiver runs down my spine. Since Dad passed away and my brothers and I assumed the roles of co-alphas, the pressure to mate and have kids has increased tenfold. More so to me since I'm the oldest—and let's be honest, the most responsible. But the idea of having kids always seemed like a distant future. Tonight, the possibility feels real, concrete. It must be Dante's strange unfinished painting getting to me.

Suddenly, a suspicion sprouts in my head. "Hey, Mom. Can you check if Dante has been hexed somehow?"

"Hexed?" Mom raises an eyebrow. "Where is that coming from?"

"If his compulsion to paint doesn't come from a vision, what other explanation could there be besides a hex?"

Mom turns to Dante once more and stares at him, deep in thought. Only when the shrill ringtone of her phone cuts the silence does she jolt back to the here and now. She walks to the table and retrieves the device.

"Dr. Mervina speaking." She listens to the caller with a solemn expression, then replies, "Are you sure?" Another pause before she continues. "Okay, I'll be there as fast as I can."

"What happened?" I ask as soon as she ends the call.

"That was Carol. The Midnight Coven showed up at her doorstep with grave news."

"What news?"

"They believe a curse or spell has been cast over all of Crimson Hollow. Carol didn't get into details over the phone, but she needs me there as soon as possible."

A sliver of apprehension pierces my chest. I can't help but wonder if Dante's peculiar behavior is a result of such a spell.

"What about Dante?"

"You put him in this state, so you'll deal with him when he

wakes up. Just don't let him return to his studio before I get back."

"Maybe whatever spell was cast over Crimson Hollow is what's wrong with him."

"We'll see."

Mom is out the door without a glance back. Her attitude rubs me the wrong way. She didn't seem that worried about Carol's call or the implications.

Damn it. I don't like this at all.

I look at my watch. It's already past one in the morning. The chances I'll hit the pillow any time soon are slim. But even if I could, I doubt I'd be able to fall asleep. I have a bad feeling, which in itself is enough to put me in a sour mood. Hunches and premonitions are Dante's department, not mine.

Putting my hands on my hips, I glower at him. The idiot is completely out to the world and has now started to snore. Ah, fuck it. I'm waking him up now.

I shake his shoulder. "Dante. Wake up."

He mumbles something and bats my hand away. I head for the sink in the room and fill a basin with ice-cold water.

"You asked for it," I say just before I dump it all over his head.

With a loud gasp, he sits up at once. "What? Where am I?"

"You're in the infirmary, Picasso."

Dante wipes his face and turns to me. "Son of a bitch. You sucker punched me."

"Yeah, yeah. Sue me. I had to get you out of that studio."

He jumps off the bed. "I have to get back. I need to finish the painting."

I grab his arm. "You're not going anywhere, brother."

He peels his lips back, revealing his sharp fangs. "Let me go," he growls.

"Not a chance."

"You don't understand. I have to finish that painting."

"You've been trying for three weeks! I'm not going to let you waste away like that."

"What am I supposed to do? I need to know who that woman in the painting is, Tristan. It's a matter of life or death."

His eyes are round and frantic, but I believe his words completely.

"Mom just received an urgent call from Carol Kane. It seems there's something witchy going on in town, and I bet your need to finish that painting is linked to the witches' emergency."

I was hoping my news would convince Dante to forget about the stupid painting, but it does the complete opposite. He yanks his arm free and bolts out of the room.

"Dante! Come back here!"

I run after him, but he's faster than me. When I step outside the building, Dante is already in midshift. Great. I have to shift as well if I hope to catch up with him.

Shakes run through my body as my muscles begin to expand and change shape. But before I can let my wolf free, bright headlights illuminate the path ahead. A car is coming down the road fast. Everything happens in a split second. Dante completely ignores the speeding vehicle and crosses in front of it.

"Dante!" I scream too late.

Tires screech as the driver attempts to stop and avoid the collision. A loud thump and Dante's whelp follow. I stop the shift, but my wolf cries, begging to be set free. I can't let him though. I have to maintain my human form if I have any hope of not killing whoever is driving the car that ran over my brother.

## 8

SAMUEL

My spine goes rigid when I hear the sound of another wolf growling. I drop my arm from the beautiful woman's shoulders and step forward, positioning myself in front of her. But my protective demeanor changes when my eyes collide with the petite woman between Kenya and Zeke. She's the one with lips peeled back and canines on display, the wolf who's about to pounce.

I didn't know she was a shifter. How is that possible?

She moves forward, but Kenya holds her arm. "Red, no."

The world goes off-kilter. Out of nowhere, something strange happens to me, almost as if there's an invisible cord pulling me toward her. First there was the tug when I saw her picture, and now this.

I lean forward, ready to breach the distance between us. But the feeling subsides when my companion, the girl I picked up at Five-Headed Dragon, hooks her arm around mine.

"Come on, Sam. It's cold, and I can't wait to check your place out."

I look into her eyes, and my thoughts become all fuzzy. The

world around us is muted. I can only see the woman staring back at me clearly.

"Step away from him, bitch, or you'll lose a limb," a female voice warns. It takes me a second to recognize it, but then it hits me. It's Red.

The fog in my brain is lifted and I'm able to look away from my date. Red steps forward, despite Kenya's hold on her arm, and then I see her round belly. My eyes stay glued to her abdomen almost as if I'm in a trance. Dizziness hits me all of a sudden. I press the heel of my hand against my forehead and close my eyes for a second.

"Shit. What's wrong with Sam?" Kenya asks.

"It's Alecto," a masculine voice answers.

I open my eyes, trying to see through my now blurry vision. A tall man steps in front of Red and the others, wearing golden armor. I blink several times to make sure I'm not seeing things.

"Fuck a duck," Zeke mutters.

"You again, Pegasus? You're such a pest. I think it's time you leave this town for good."

A flaming dagger appears in my companion's hand. Instinctively, I leap away from her. "What the hell!"

"Don't worry, pet. It'll only be a moment."

An invisible blanket wraps around my body, rendering me paralyzed. I should get the hell away from this crazy creature, but it's like my body has a mind of its own. I'm unable to move, and my brain feels like it's been scrambled.

The tall stranger begins to shimmer until he changes into a white horse with golden wings. My wolf churns inside my core, but my connection to him seems muffled somehow.

Alarm bells ring in my head. There's never been a time when my link to the wolf was weak.

Alecto charges the magical horse with a battle cry, and I can't look away. But a sharp pain in the back of my head knocks me over. I fall to my knees, ready to retaliate, when Zeke appears in front of me and touches my forehead.

That's the last thing I see.

---

RED

Everything happens in a flash. While Pegasus and Alecto are busy fighting each other, Zeke knocks Samuel down with his imp powers and tosses him over his shoulder, and we escape.

We run back to Zeke's bakery, but he rounds the corner. A few seconds later, I understand the reason. Without stopping, he opens the back door of his delivery van and tosses an unconscious Samuel on the floor.

"Careful with him," I say before jumping inside.

"Maybe you should ride shotgun, Red," Kenya suggests.

"No!" I snap, not knowing where the rage came from. "I'll sit with him."

"Come on, Kenya. Get in!" Zeke says from behind the wheel. "Pegasus will only be able to distract Alecto for so long. We have to get out of here."

Kenya jumps inside and then closes the van's back door, but with Sam sprawled on the floor, there's little room for her to move forward. The situation doesn't improve when Zeke peels out of the parking spot, the lurch sending Kenya flying to the side.

"Fuck!" she exclaims when she hits her hip against a storage cabinet.

"Sorry, cookie. You'd better come sit in front with me and buckle up."

Clutching the cabinet, she inches forward. Before she crosses to the front seat, she glances at me. "You can't stay on the floor with Sam, Red. It's not safe."

The van swerves sharply in that moment, almost sending Kenya down. Instead of listening to her words, I scooch closer to Samuel and prop his head on my lap. "I'm fine here. Go take a seat before you fly out the window."

Grumbling, she slides through the small gap between the two seats at the front and drops down hard when Zeke's manic driving skills force her to.

"Jeez, forget that fucking goddess. We won't survive this trip," she complains.

"Can Alecto find us regardless of where we go?" I ask.

"Zeke Mobile is protected. She won't find us easily."

"Only if she were blind. This van is like a neon parade float. Astronauts can see us from outer space," Kenya retorts.

"That's why I'm trying to get as far as I can from that psycho bitch," Zeke grits out.

"Do we have a plan? Where are we going?" I ask.

"To the Wolfe compound. It's closest to us, and hopefully your other mates are there."

Samuel mumbles on my lap, fidgeting in his sleep. Impulsively, I run my fingers through his hair. An electric current goes up my arm, catching me by surprise. I feel another kick in my belly, almost as if my baby is reacting to the contact as well.

I stare unabashedly at him, something easy to do now since he's out to the world. I've seen him before in town—at least, that's the current memory I have in my mind. He's so handsome, it's almost impossible to believe I'm mated to him.

He becomes more agitated, and his face twists into a scowl. Taken over by another impulse, I lean forward and kiss his forehead. When I pull back, my face bursts into flames. Samuel is awake and staring at me.

"I'm sorry," I blurt out. He doesn't answer right away. Instead he keeps staring at me with his striking electric blue eyes. "What?"

He sits up and twists his body so he can keep looking into my eyes. "Who are you?"

"Is Sam awake?" Kenya asks from the front seat.

I should answer her, but I'm tongue-tied and nervous. I'm torn between moving away from this stranger or throwing myself into his arms. My heart is thundering inside of my chest, and my mouth is dry.

"You kidnapped me," Samuel continues.

"Technically, we saved your ass," Zeke pipes up.

Sam turns to the front of the van. "Where are you taking me?"

"To your mother. Oh shit, hold on. Sharp curve ahead."

Zeke's warning is moot. With the way we're speeding, it only came half a second before he actually turns the bend and sends me flying forward. Sam catches me in his arms, but I still hit my belly too hard against his body. I let out a grunt.

"Are you okay?" he asks, easing me off him to peer worriedly into my eyes.

My heart skips a beat, only to take off in a mad race in the next second. An avalanche of emotions hits me all at once, and I don't know what do with all the foreign and overwhelming feelings.

"Red?" he probes when I don't answer him.

I snap out of my haze and glance down. "I'm okay. I just hit my belly a little too hard."

"So you're really pregnant," he says in awe while staring at it.

"Apparently so, even if I don't remember how I got like this."

"Well, I can think of several ways," he replies with humor before glancing at me from under his eyelashes.

*Mamma mia.* He's smiling at me with full dimples on display. I'm glad I'm already on the floor, because my legs are jelly now.

"May I touch it?" he asks.

"Huh?" I reply, sounding stupid as fuck. *Ugh. What's wrong with me?*

"Your belly. May I touch it?"

I nod, unable to form words. He places his hand right on my abdomen, and once again I sense a strange exchange of energy between us. He sucks in a breath and stares at me wide-eyed.

"I felt a kick." He glances down again. "Another one. Holy smokes, how many babies do you have in there?"

"Three," Kenya replies before I can.

"What?" I squeak. "You're joking, right?"

She turns in her seat to stare at me. "No, honey, I'm not. You're a triplex."

Samuel pulls his hand away suddenly and looks at me with a peculiar glint in his eyes. "I'm one of triplets."

I open my mouth to tell him I know when Kenya screams, "Watch out!"

Zeke presses on the brakes so suddenly that Samuel and I slide forward on the floor at terrible speed. I only have time for one thought: *my babies*.

## 9

## TRISTAN

"No!" The scream that erupts from my throat is almost not human. I halted the shift, but my wolf is still churning.

I cut the distance between myself and the van at breakneck speed. I don't have a visual of Dante anymore, which only makes my fear ten times worse. The driver is already out of the vehicle before I get to him. I only catch a mop of white-blond hair, but it's enough to recognize Zeke. I leap on him, sending the imp and myself to the ground. I'm going to kill the motherfucker. With fangs bared, I growl, straddling him.

"Get off me, Tristan!" He grabs my arms, trying to dislodge me.

A woman screams nearby, and that gives me pause. I look over my shoulder and see Kenya standing not too far from us.

"Stop it, Tristan! It wasn't his fault." She turns, dropping in a crouch next to an unmoving white form. Dante.

I jump off the imp and veer toward my brother. But when a new scent reaches my nose, I freeze. It's familiar and foreign at the same time, and it ignites something in the pit of my stomach. I only catch Sam's scent a second later. He appears from behind the van with his arm wrapped around a blonde woman's shoulder.

I suck in a breath as the sense of familiarity increases. I know her. But from where?

A whine catches my attention, and I force my gaze from the mysterious woman in Sam's arm and turn to Dante. Crouching next to Kenya, I touch his pelt. "You stupid wolf."

"I think Zeke only nicked one of his hind legs," Kenya says. "He came out of nowhere."

"Why were you speeding inside the compound like that?" I peer over my shoulder to glower at Zeke.

"Because I like to pretend I'm a Formula One driver in my spare time. What do you think? We have an emergency." He approaches, returning the angry stare.

"Congratulations. You just added another one," I snap.

"Is he going to be okay?" the girl with Sam asks, sending chills down my spine. God, I've never reacted like that in the presence of any wo—

Wait a second.

I take another deep breath and realize she's not human. She's a wolf.

Dante springs back on his four paws—well, three—and stares at the unfamiliar shifter. He then turns his nose up and howls.

Kenya unfurls from her crouch, eyeing the girl with worry. "Red, are you okay?"

"I'm fi—" She hisses, closing her eyes.

"Shit. What is it? Are the babies okay?" Sam stares wide-eyed at her protruding belly. Not only is she a wolf shifter but a knocked-up one. My heart squeezes painfully at the sight. I want to take her in my arms and protect her at all costs. What a bizarre reaction to a mere stranger.

"I told you to buckle up, silly girl. Sam, take her inside ASAP. We need Dr. Mervina," Kenya states.

"I'm fine, Kenya. One of the babies just kicked me in the ribs."

As if she hadn't spoken, Sam picks her up in his arms and strides toward the manor. Dante follows close on their heels, hopping a little thanks to his injured leg. I want to go with them, but I fight the urge because it's damn crazy.

"What's the emergency?" I ask Kenya instead.

"We'd better go inside. There's no telling who's listening."

Her reply is ominous, and it only adds to my growing alarm. I think about Dante's erratic behavior and the witches' emergency that took Mom away from the compound.

Shit, that's right. She's not home. What if Red needs medical attention?

Before I know it, I'm sprinting toward the house.

"It took him long enough" I hear Zeke say, but his comment isn't important right now.

Once inside the house, Sam's already set Red down on one of the couches and is now fawning over her.

"Can I get you something? Food, water?"

"No, I'm fine."

Now that I can have a good look at her under proper illumination, I notice she's not wearing much in terms of clothing. I'm irritated in an instant. "You went out like that? It's freezing."

She levels me with a glare, and it hits me straight in the chest. It also makes my libido skyrocket. For fuck's sake. Now is not the time for an unwanted erection.

"I didn't have anything to wear."

"What do you mean, you didn't have anything to wear?" I ask.

"It means this"—she points at her pregnant belly—"is a new development. Like less than twenty-four hours new."

"Come again?"

"Whoa." Kenya raises her hand. "Everyone take a chill pill and let me explain what's going on."

Dante begins to shimmer and shake, drawing Red's attention to him. "Oh my God. What's happening to the wolf?"

"He's shifting. Why are you acting like you don't know? You're a shifter," I say.

She blinks fast, almost as if she's having a hard time processing my words. Then she turns to the sheriff's daughter. "Kenya? What is he talking about?"

Dante finishes his shift and stands naked in front of our visitors. Not that shifters care about that, but Kenya averts her gaze just the same.

"Oh my God," her friend murmurs.

"Dude. Put some clothes on." Sam tries to push Dante away, but he ignores our brother and drops into a crouch in front of Red.

"It's you. The woman I've been trying to paint for the last three weeks."

"Why were you trying to paint me? I-I don't know you."

Zeke turns to Kenya. "Are you thinking what I'm thinking?"

"Jeez, I don't know, Zeke. I'm not a Vulcan. I can't read minds."

"Dante is a psychic of sorts. Maybe the Furies' spell doesn't quite work on him."

"Wait a second. Whose spell?" I ask.

"The Furies, the three goddesses of vengeance. They're here in Crimson Hollow, and they're after you," Red replies with fear in her eyes.

"Why would some crazy-ass goddesses be after us?" Sam asks.

Dante sits on the balls of his feet and sags his shoulders. "I used to know the answer to that. Why can't I remember now?"

"Because the Furies wiped everyone's memories. Well, everyone's besides mine and Zeke's," Kenya answers.

"Okay, let me get this straight. So, I got my memory wiped

clean. Then how come I remember every single thing that happened to me in the last week? Month?" I ask.

"The memories you have right now aren't real," Zeke replies.

I turn to the blonde woman on the couch again. It seems I can't keep my eyes off her for too long. A nagging suspicion presents itself.

"And who are you exactly?" I ask her.

She takes a deep breath before she replies, "Apparently, I'm your mate."

"*My* mate?" My voice rises a fraction while my heart jump-starts. It seems the stupid muscle agrees with that notion.

"Not only *your* mate. The three of you." She lowers her gaze, almost as if she's embarrassed.

"But that's impossible," Sam chimes in.

"Okay, we don't have time for you to process the news. Red is mated to the three of you, and she's expecting a few pups. The most important thing to focus on right now is the fact that you have three psycho deities hell-bent on getting revenge on your asses," Kenya interjects.

"And how do we stop them and get our memories back?" I ask.

Zeke opens his mouth to reply, but the manor's front door explodes inward, sending shards of broken wood everywhere. On instinct, I jump in front of Red to protect her from the blast. My brothers are overcome with the same instinct, and together we end up forming a human cocoon around the girl.

But as much as I'd like to keep protecting her, I need to face whoever burst in through the door like that. I turn around with fangs bared and clawed hands.

Two tall women stand in front of the gaping hole where the door used to be. They're dressed like Amazon warriors with plated bodices and metal harnesses around their forearms. Even if they weren't dressed like that, it would be impossible to miss the power rolling off their frames in waves. They must be two of the Furies.

"How dare you invade my home?" I growl while my brothers stand on each side of me. I don't fucking care if they're goddesses or not.

"Silence, mortal! You won't speak to us like that." The woman with long ebony hair and dark skin flicks her wrist and there's a sudden pressure around my throat. I try to speak, but nothing comes out.

*What the fuck!*

"He's not one of her wolves. Let's just turn him into dust," the second Fury says with glee.

"You're not turning anyone into dust. I won't allow it." Red walks around us and positions herself as a protective barrier. Her shoulders are squared back, her chin lifted high.

*Is she crazy?*

My brothers and I all move forward to get Red out of harm's way when her entire body begins to glow a blue light.

"Oh, look at that. The she-wolf thinks she can use her puny magic to fight us, Tisy."

"Come on, ladies. There's no reason to get carried away." Zeke moves forward with his hands up. "You had your fun. Now why wo—"

The dark-haired Fury waves her hand and sends the imp flying across the room. He hits the far wall and drops like a sack of potatoes. Kenya gasps, covering her mouth with her hands.

The glow around Red intensifies, and I sense she's about to do something foolish. I'd tell her to stop if I had a voice.

"Red, don't do it," Dante pleads.

"Listen to the little wolf, Red. Unless you want to truly piss us off."

"Leave my friend alone," Kenya warns. "Your beef is with Artemis, so why are you here?"

"We don't answer to the likes of you, demon spawn," the second Fury sneers.

*Demon spawn? What is she talking about now?*

Kenya freezes completely, and it takes me a moment to realize she didn't do it out of fear. Red runs to her friend, stopping in front of her to clutch her shoulders. "Kenya!" She shakes the girl, but she's stiff as a board.

"What the hell did you do to her?" Sam asks.

"She was annoying," Tisy replies. "Hmm, but I'm not happy with her punishment." She flicks her wrist, and Kenya shrinks into a small plastic figurine.

Red covers her mouth and suppresses a sob.

"I'm bored. I think it's time we crank things up a notch." The second Fury raises her hand, fingers poised to snap. Instinctively, I know the moment she does, our situation will change from bad to worse.

Out in the distance, I hear the sound of several wolves howling. The pack's enforcers are approaching. Both goddesses turn toward the gap they made, taking their eyes off us for a moment. Red drops into a crouch and swoops miniature Kenya into her hand. Without stopping to think, I grab Red's arm and run in the opposite direction. It's clear we can't fight those deities alone, and my instinct is to protect Red at all costs.

My brothers follow us, but we don't get far.

"Where do you think you're going?" one of the Furies asks, and then Red is yanked from my grasp.

She screams. I whirl around just in time to watch her disappear into thin air.

"No!" my brothers yell at the same time, while my scream gets stuck in my throat.

"You bitch," Dante grits out, already in midshift as he charges

The Furies smile wickedly, but there's no sense trying to stop him. It's too late. He leaps and then the entire scene vanishes.

I jolt into a sitting position in bed with my heart thundering. I rub my face while I grasp at the tendrils of the most vivid nightmare I've had in days. The room is still dark, and a quick glance at my cell tells me it's only three in the morning.

The sound of sheets rubbing together catches my attention. A hand touches my arm. "Tristan? Is everything okay?"

The lamp turns on, revealing Lyria's worried face staring at me. My heart clenches so tightly it hurts. Why is looking at her giving me such chest pains? We've been dating for a while, but I can't remember when we got together.

"Yeah, I'm fine. Just a nightmare."

She runs her hand over my abs. "Why don't you lie down and I'll make you forget all about it."

Goose bumps spread all over my skin, and not the good kind.

"I think I'm going for a run." I jump out of bed.

"Right now? It's the middle of the night and it's snowing."

I look out the window, getting a full view of the main square. Not a soul in sight. "You know the cold doesn't bother me."

"Do you want company?" She makes a motion to get out of bed too.

"No, go back to sleep. I won't be long."

Her eyebrows furrow together, almost as if she doesn't like my answer. "Tristan, you're worrying me."

"Nothing to worry about, babe." The endearment feels sour in my mouth. "I just need to clear my head."

Before she can offer another argument, I slip out of the room. All I grab before I head out is my coat hanging by the front door. I don't even put my shoes on. The need to get out of my own apartment is urgent and disturbing at the same time.

## 10

### RED

THE FIRST THING THAT COMES BACK TO ME IS MY HEARING. TOO bad all I can hear is the sound of my pulse beating in my ears. Then comes the freezing cold, but not the regular low temperature of a winter's night. This sensation is different, soul deep.

I finally open my eyes, and it's not the sky of Crimson Hollow that greets me. It's something foreign. It's not night, but it's also not day. There's no sun or moon, only an endless number of clouds in a gray sky.

I'm lying on rough ground, and when I try to move, I end up piercing my palm on the hard surface. I sit up and realize I'm surrounded by small pebbles that are as sharp as razors. Looking around, I see nothing but a bare landscape stretching out before me. My stomach bottoms out and my heart clenches tightly in my chest. I have no idea where I am, but I'm definitely not home anymore.

On unsteady legs, I get up. At once, my bladder complains. I guess mortal peril doesn't mean shit to Mother Nature. I amble toward the trunk of a lonely, dying tree. I don't see a living soul for miles, so I do the only thing I can at the moment—I pull my leggings down and squat, using the tree as support.

Once that's taken care of, I pull my jacket closer together and begin to walk in a random direction. I've never felt so lonely in my entire life, but I can't succumb to the urge to cry. I have to be strong, if not for me then for the babies I'm carrying.

I cover my belly with my hands, needing to feel a kick for the first time since I woke up without my memories. But the babies are quiet now. I hope they're okay. If something happens to them, I'll tear the Furies limb from limb, even if I have to die in the process.

The feeling of protectiveness fills me with much-needed motivation. A warmth concentrates in my chest before spreading throughout my body. It helps against the chill, and it also gives me physical strength. Suddenly, my senses are enhanced; I can hear sounds that I couldn't before. It's faint, but I catch the constant clattering of metal and the murmurs of a crowd. There's some type of civilization ahead, over the hill.

I take a big whiff and catch several scents in the air, none pleasant. Whatever is waiting for me might not be what I'm hoping for. But I don't have a choice. Sitting here in the desert won't get me home.

The picture of the house Zeke took me to, the Alpha Manor, comes to the forefront of my mind. That's what my brain immediately produced when I thought about home. Could I be recovering my memories already? I can't deny my connection to the three Wolfe brothers. The pull was there, and the feeling that I knew them was strong.

*They're my mates.*

The realization hits me at once. It's a certainty that can't be refuted or ignored. And yet I can't remember them. I have no memory of when we met, when we fell in love. Sadness immediately washes over me, followed swiftly by anger. Those damn Furies erased my life, separated me from my mates, and because of what? Their petty vendetta against Artemis, another asshole deity.

I'm so wrapped up in my fury that I don't realize how fast I'm going. Only when my breathing begins to come out in bursts do I return to the present moment. I've reached the top of the hill, and from my new vantage point, I have the visual of a great market. Hundreds of dark brown tents are clustered together, and crisscrossing the area are narrow walking paths filled with creatures. Instinctively, I know they aren't humans. From where I stand they look like tiny ants moving at a snail's pace.

At the edge of the market, shoddy-looking buildings stand precariously. They're one storm away from collapsing. This is the closest to civilization I'll get, it seems, so I might as well head down there and find help.

I tense as soon as the idea enters my head. My body freezes.

*Come on, Red. Now is not the time to get a panic attack.*

The inner pep talk does little to dissuade the fear that entered my heart. I don't know where the sudden emotion is coming from. The hill is much steeper from this side; I bet that's the reason. I search for a path to go down but find nothing. *Great.* I guess I'll have to climb down the hard way. It wouldn't be so bad if I wasn't about to pop out a litter of puppies.

I snort inwardly. I'm already starting to think about them as little wolves. This is crazy. Couldn't those fucking goddesses at least let me keep the knowledge that I'm a wolf shifter? The guys know who they are, after all.

Wishful thinking, of course. The little I know about deities is that they're all a bunch of psychos.

Careful not to lose my balance, I bend my knees and lean against the rocky surface sideways. At least the hill isn't made out of razor-sharp material like the place I landed. Slowly, I slide down, careful where I place my feet. I'm glad I'm wearing snow boots with non-slippery soles.

It takes me several minutes to go down. I'm maybe a yard from the bottom when I put my foot on a loose rock. It shifts under me, and there goes my precarious balance. I slide down the rest of the way. My fall lasts less than a few seconds, but when I finally stop, the side of my leg is screaming. Grunting, I push myself to a sitting position. No wonder I'm in so much pain. I scratched the side of my thigh raw. The flimsy fabric of my leggings didn't stand a chance; parts of the skin have completely peeled off, and it's now oozing blood.

I'm debating whether I should unwrap the scarf from my neck and tie it around my leg when the growling from a wild animal sounds from not too far behind me. My heart drops to the pit of my stomach. Slowly, I look over my shoulder and see a creature straight out of a nightmare. I don't know what it is, a cross between a hyena and an alligator perhaps. But one thing is clear: it wants to make a meal out of me.

I jump to my feet quickly without losing my balance again—a feat that shocks me considering I'm a whale—and take off at a run toward the buildings that surround the market. The monster makes a guttural noise and gives chase. I don't need to look to know; I can hear its weirdly shaped paws hitting the hard ground.

The burst of energy that I felt earlier hits me again. The power is too foreign and wild; it has to be the wolf inside of me. I wish I could shift, but I don't know how or even if I can in my condition. But no matter how fast I can now run on two legs, I'm not fast enough to outrun whatever is chasing me.

Its hideous noises are getting closer.

I'm almost at the first building when the creature snaps its alligator jaws and bites the end of my coat. The fabric tears but not completely, and I'm yanked back. I end up stepping in a hole and hear a snap followed by white-hot pain in my left ankle. The fall is inevitable. Somehow, I manage to contort my torso so I don't collapse belly first. Instead, my right arm and shoulder take the brunt of the impact.

I try to turn into a ball to protect my babies from the attack that's sure to come, but instead of sharp jaws piercing my skin, I hear a pitchy whine followed by the feel of warm blood splattering over me. Through the pounding in my ears, I can also distinguish the sound of boots crunching loose gravel.

I'm not alone anymore.

Rolling over, I uncover my face to see what's going on. There's a petite hooded figure hunched over the carcass of the beast that was about to devour me. Muttering curses under her breath, she yanks a spear from the back of the monster and then turns to me. Her face is partially hidden in shadows; I can only see her chin and hard-set mouth.

With bloody spear in hand, she moves in my direction. Fuck. Just because she killed the monster doesn't mean she's friendly. I'm caught between scooching back and trying to get up. Shit, this is the most ungraceful attempt at escaping.

"Don't come any closer," I warn.

The stranger stops, pulling her hood back. An Asian woman with a long dark braid draped over her shoulder stares at me. She looks human, but my senses tell me she isn't.

"Red? What the hell are you doing here?"

"You know who I am?"

Squinting, she places her hands on her hips. "Did you hit your head or something?"

"No. I was cursed by the three vengeful bitches."

The woman offers me her hand, and since I don't feel any threat coming from her, I take it. She grunts as she pulls me up. "Jeez, how heavy are you? Aren't you close to your due date?"

I pull my hand free from her grasp and hug myself. "You seem to know a lot about me. Who are you?"

"You really don't know?" She cocks her head to the side.

"No."

"I'm Nina Ogata, fox spy extraordinaire." She curls her lips in a lopsided grin.

"You're a fox?" I squeak.

She chuckles. "Shit. If you don't who I am, and you wound up here in the Wastelands, then it means you're in a heap of trouble. Your mates must be going crazy."

A sharp pain pierces my chest. "Not likely. We've all been cursed. They don't remember me, and I don't remember them."

"Shit. Who did this to you? Artemis?"

I shake my head. "No. The Furies."

Nina's eyes go rounder. "Son of a bitch. You're really fucked."

11

---

DANTE

I MUST HAVE SPACED OUT FOR A MOMENT, BECAUSE THE TWO potential customers standing in front of me have expectant expressions on their faces. They probably asked me something.

"I'm sorry. Could you please repeat that?" I ask.

"We wanted to know if you miss living in West Virginia," the bald man with thick black-rimmed glasses replies.

His question gives me pause. I've been living in New York City for the past six months, and it's the first time the thought of my hometown gives me nostalgia. When my father passed away, Tristan assumed the role of the pack's alpha. In theory, we all should be sharing the responsibility to lead the pack, but the reality is Tristan was the one born to rule. Sam has the band, and I have my art. Since the first time I picked up a paintbrush, I knew that's what I'd be doing for the rest of my life.

"Yes, as a matter of fact, I do," I say, surprising myself.

I feel a prickly sensation on the back of my neck. It stirs my wolf awake. Something isn't right here. I glance around the art gallery. It's a successful opening, and the place is full. I should be rejoicing that all these people came to see my paintings, but the sense of foreboding won't leave me alone.

"Do you plan to return soon?" the guy's wife asks.

"As a matter of fact—"

"No, Dante is not going anywhere in the near future," a female voice answers from behind me.

I turn to find Tisy, the gallery owner and the woman responsible for my relocation to the Big Apple. She came into my gallery in Crimson Hollow six months ago and fell in love with my work. She invited me to come to the city to broaden my horizons, and surprisingly, I accepted her proposal right away. Never mind that life for a wolf shifter in a big city is way more complicated. I didn't give much thought of how peculiar my decision was until tonight.

Tisy laces her arm with mine and pats my chest. She's always been affectionate like that, and she's never hidden the fact that she's attracted to me. But I've always kept her at arm's length, too busy with painting to even entertain the idea of sleeping with anyone. But I know tonight Tisy expects more, and an hour ago, I was more than ready to entertain her. But now, there's this nagging feeling that something is off, and I'm less than enthusiastic to spend the night with her.

My vision goes out of focus for a split second, and then I get a flash migraine. Shit. I'm about to have a vision. I haven't had one in over a year, so I'm definitely due. But I can't let it happen in front of all these people, especially in front of Tisy.

"It was nice meeting you, Mr. and Mrs. Summers. If you excuse me, I have to make the rounds."

I try to unhook my arm from Tisy's, but she keeps her hold. "I'll come with you."

"I actually need to go to the restroom first." I finally break free.

I cut across the room in large strides to make sure Tisy doesn't follow me. I wouldn't put it past the woman; I can smell her arousal from miles away. As I walk toward the back of the gallery, the eerie sensation increases. When I reach the empty hallway that leads to the restrooms, I have the feeling someone is spying on me. I whirl around, certain I'd find a person there, but there's no one.

Another painful throb in my forehead renders me blind for a second. Pressing the heel of my hand against it, I take deep breaths to ride out the pain. My eyesight returns, but the world around me vanishes into the background. The image of a blonde woman wearing a red gown appears before me. A yearning like I've never known hits me hard, robbing me of breath.

This is a vision, but I don't feel the itching to paint. No, the overwhelming compulsion is to get the hell out of here and find her.

Her image vanishes abruptly and standing before me is a tall blond man instead. Not a vision this time. He's beaten up and bleeding from a cut above his eyebrow. In an instant, I know he's not human. It's not because of what he's wearing—golden knight armor—but the aura surrounding him.

"Who are you?" I ask.

He crosses the distance between us. "Dante, we don't have much time. You have to come with me." He reaches for my arm, but the wolf's instinct takes over. I leap out of his reach, ready to let my wild side free.

"I don't know who you are, but I'll only give you one warning. Get the fuck out before I turn you into shreds."

He looks over his shoulder and his entire body becomes tenser. "Damn it. She's coming." He turns to me again, eyes frantic. "You're in grave danger. If you don't come with me, Tisy will make sure you'll never see your family again."

"What are you talking about?"

"No time to explain." He throws his arm forward, and a golden lasso whips out, wrapping around me.

My muscles spasm as I'm blasted with a shock wave so

powerful I end up biting my tongue. The metallic taste of cooper fills my mouth. Son of a bitch.

The last thing I see is Tisy running toward us with a murderous expression on her face. Then a vortex of light surrounds me, spinning so rapidly that I have to close my eyes or risk throwing up.

The electric shocks cease, but it's another minute before the whirling does as well.

I hit the ground with a loud thud, but the fall isn't that jarring. I landed on a grassy field if the intense smell of earth and green is any indication. When I blink my eyes open, the bright blue sky of a summer day greets me.

*What the hell?*

My muscles are still sore from the electrocution, but I'm able to jump to my feet. With claws exposed and fangs bared, I turn around, looking for the motherfucker who brought me here. I'm in a beautifully manicured garden, and the sense of déjà vu hits me like a cannonball.

I've been here before.

There's no sign of the guy, but a familiar scent leads me forward. Birds chirp away, and on my path, I spot deer eating grass lazily and bunnies hopping in a playful manner. The animals don't even glance in my direction. Can't they sense the wolf in me?

When I turn the bend, I get the visual of a white pergola wrapped in vines and flowers. Under it is a white chaise lounge with colorful pillows. Flashes of long-forgotten memories appear before my eyes. I remember sitting by that piece of furniture as a wolf. Sam was also there.

"Dante?" a velvety female voice asks from behind me.

I whirl on the spot, and at once, I know who she is. "Artemis."

"What are you doing here?" She approaches me with caution, then peers over my shoulder.

"I don't know."

"Who brought you here?" She narrows her eyes to slits while a powerful energy surrounds her.

The answer comes to me like I had always known it. "Pegasus."

"That meddling, arrogant idiot!" Artemis throws her head back and yells, "Pegasus!"

One, two beats pass before the golden knight shimmers into view. He's kneeling and breathing hard. He's also bleeding more. Someone gave him an ass whooping.

"Shit," I cross the distance between us and then bend over to help him up. "What the hell happened to you?"

He lifts his chin, meeting my gaze. "You recovered your memories. I was hoping that bringing you here would do the trick."

"Recover my memories? I don't know what you're talking about."

His face twists into a grimace as I lift him up. "You don't remember your mate, Red?"

"My mate?"

"You're a moron, Pegasus," Artemis chimes in. "Dante only remembers this place because he was born here, and despite his betrayal, he's still bound to me in a way."

I rub the back of my neck, feeling truly at a loss. "What's going on?"

"The Furies broke free from their prison in the Underworld, and they took their revenge on you," Pegasus replies.

Brow furrowing, I turn to Artemis, the goddess to whom I was bound many millennia ago. Somehow, we parted ways, but I can't remember how. Still, the sting of betrayal hurts. "And you didn't do anything?"

She juts out her chin. "Why should I? You left me for the mortal girl."

The image of a beautiful blonde woman flashes in my

mind again, followed by excruciating pain. I massage my temple and say, "I can't remember her. Why can't I remember her?"

"The Furies took that away from you, though I'm not sure what they hope to accomplish from it. It seems every time you get close to recovering your real memories, they interfere and give you new made-up ones."

"Are you saying I didn't actually move to New York?"

Artemis snorts. "You're a wolf, Dante. Wolves don't do well in big cities. I can't believe you didn't see right through their bullshit illusion."

"Where is my mate now?"

Pegasus's expression falls. "The Furies sent her to another dimension. I haven't been to locate her yet."

A terrible ache flares in my chest, almost as if someone pierced me with a dagger.

"It's because you're nothing but a pesky pet." Artemis scoffs.

*Shit. If Pegasus, Zeus's chosen champion, is a 'pesky pet,' then what am I?*

"Do you know were my mate is?" I ask.

Artemis stares at me with a calculating gleam in her eyes. "I do."

I take a step forward. "Where is she?"

Her brow furrows, and a flash of anger reflects in her gaze. "You don't even remember her, yet you suffer by not knowing her fate."

"Her memory might have been scrubbed from my brain, but it hasn't been removed from my heart."

"Nothing can keep you apart, can't it?" Artemis laughs derisively.

"No."

A lonely tear rolls down her cheek. She wipes it off hastily and looks over my shoulder. "Why did you bring him here, Pegasus? To taunt me with what I've lost?"

"No. To remind you that you still care for your wolves. You can stop the Furies, Artemis."

She shakes her head. "No. I can't. Why do think I had Hades imprison them in the first place?"

"So, that's it? You're just going to let those three bitches have their revenge?" Pegasus raises his voice.

"What would you have me do? Return to the human realm and challenge them to a fight?"

I don't know where the certainty comes from, but I know a fight between Artemis and the Furies in Crimson Hollow will level the town to the ground.

"You can start by telling me where my mate is," I grit out.

Artemis stares at me with a solemn and hard expression. "She's in the Wastelands."

There's another clench in my chest. Wherever that is, it's not a good place. "How come that name sounds familiar?"

"You've been there before," Pegasus replies. "We have to hurry. Red isn't safe."

"Can you take me?"

He opens his mouth to reply, but nothing comes from him but a hiss. He leans forward, clutching his chest.

"What is it?" I ask.

"It's my father. He's learned of Pegasus's shenanigans and is calling him back home." Artemis scoffs.

In the next moment, Zeus's champion disappears, leaving me alone with the goddess I betrayed. It doesn't matter that I don't recall how. I remember everything about Artemis, and she's not the forgiving type.

"I need to save my mate," I tell her.

"I know." A glass of red wine appears in her hand out of thin air. She takes a sip from it without taking her eyes off me.

"Are you going to make me beg?"

"Tempting, but no. As much as it pains me to admit defeat, I lost your heart to the human girl for good. Seeing you humiliate yourself at my feet so you can run to her rescue will only rub the wound raw."

"Then what?"

"I can send you to the Wastelands, but once you're there, you'll have to find a way out yourself. It won't be easy."

"I'll manage. Just get me there. *Please*."

"Very well." She raises her hand.

"Wait. Can you undo the memory spell the Furies cast on me?"

Artemis stares at me without blinking for several beats. I sense a soft tingling over my temple, and once the feeling vanishes, she speaks. "I'm sorry, Dante. The Furies did a number on your mind that not even I can undo."

My stomach bottoms out. If Artemis, one of the most powerful goddesses in all of Mount Olympus, can't undo the damages the Furies inflicted, what hope is there that I'll ever remember my mate?

"Don't look so distressed. They made certain I couldn't undo their spell, but they've underestimated the power of the bond of a mated wolf." Her lips curl into a sardonic grin. "Are you ready?"

"As ready as I'll ever be."

She snaps her fingers, and once again I find myself inside a damn vortex of light. The trip lasts only a few seconds, but it seems like I shattered into a million pieces and was put back together in that short amount of time. When I finally arrive at my final destination, I land on my knees, sending white-hot pain up my legs. I grunt, taking deep breaths to ride through it.

The snarling sound of a wild animal prickles my ears, making me tense in an instant. I lift my gaze and discover I'm in the middle of a barren landscape, and not too far from me is a savage creature tearing apart its latest kill.

The beast raises its ugly face in my direction and growls.

## 12

### TRISTAN

It's the middle of the night, and despite the town square being completely deserted at this hour, I don't dare to shift. I'd probably blend in with the snow as a wolf, but I can't risk being spotted by a non-supe. I settle for jogging, hoping the exercise will make me shake off this strange feeling that something is wrong.

I don't have a particular destination in my mind, just let my feet take me wherever they want to. Lost in my troubling thoughts, I don't realize I have wandered off into a seedy part of town until I reach Hell's Hole, a bar managed by a half troll where Sam and his bandmates like to hang out. I've only been inside the place once when he dragged me here. I don't get the appeal. It's a disgusting establishment frequented by the shadiest people in town. It's definitely not my scene, but I stop in front of the building just the same and debate going in. If the foreboding cloud over my head is actually a premonition, this will be the spot to gain intel.

Mind made up, I take a step forward, but the sound of fighting catches my attention. It's coming from the alleyway between the bar and another building. Letting my wolf senses expand, I pick up the scent of sulfur. *Fuck. What are demons doing here in Crimson Hollow?* The odor is faint, which means the demons nearby are at the bottom of the hellish food chain, but even so, their presence here is alarming to say the least.

"You've been a hard imp to track, Zeke," a male voice taunts before the distinct sound of a fist meeting flesh echoes in the distance.

Fuck. Of course Zeke Rogers had to be involved. There isn't such a thing as a harmless agent of Hell. I trust the guy as far as I can throw him, but like it or not, he *is* a member of Crimson Hollow's supe community. Cursing, I stride toward the putrid alleyway, stopping at the entrance.

Three beefy demons in human form are taking turns kicking and beating the shit out of the imp, who's on the ground, curled in a fetal position. My wolf stirs awake, and a growl comes from deep in my throat.

The demons stop their assault to turn in my direction.

"Ah, great, a wolf shifter," one of them mutters. "Walk away, mutt. This doesn't concern you."

I take a step forward, letting my wild essence roll off me in waves. "You're in my town, attacking a member of my community. This *does* concern me."

They forget Zeke completely and turn to me. Red eyes glow in the dark, and the guttural sounds of beasts echo around me.

"You asked for this, bitch."

One of them charges and whips a dark-clawed hand at me. I leap out of the way with ease, and not even bothering to finalize my shift, I slash my own sharp nails across the demon's neck. The gurgling sound of the creature drowning in his own blood follows.

I whirl toward the other two, ready to dispatch them back to Hell, but they seem frozen. "Who's next?"

"Fuck. You're an alpha," the demon on the right says.

"I didn't sign up to fight an alpha," the second demon replies before pivoting around and running in the opposite direction.

His companion shuffles backward, and the stench of his fear reaches me. He's going to bolt too, but before he can, a pointy object protrudes from his chest. He glances down for a brief moment, and then his legs give out from under him. He collapses into a heap and doesn't move.

Zeke is standing there with a bloody athame in hand. "Thanks for the assist, Tristan."

"If you were armed, why did you let those fuckers beat you up?" I ask.

"They caught me by surprise." Zeke wipes his blade on the back of the slain demon's jacket before the weapon disappears from view.

"Why were they after you anyway?"

The imp shakes his head. "Let's just say I pissed off the wrong demon lord. But it doesn't matter. I'm glad you found me. I was actually on my way to see you."

My spine goes taut. I've never had any business with Zeke, and the fact that he wanted to talk to me doesn't comfort me.

"Why?"

He looks over his shoulder in a cagey manner before moving closer. "Where did you wake up tonight?"

"What kind of question is that? I was in my apartment."

"Alone?"

"Why?" I narrow my eyes as suspicion licks the back of my neck.

"Just answer the question, Tristan. It's important."

"Lyria was there."

The imp's face blanches, and his eyes turn as round as saucers. "Holy fuck. I can't believe they went there."

"Who? What are you talking about?"

"Yes, Zeke. What the hell are you talking about?" Lyria asks from the other side of the alleyway.

Zeke faces her, immediately tense.

"Lyria? Did you follow me?" I ask, not hiding the irritation in my voice.

"I was worried about you, Tristan." She sashays toward us, but there's something wrong with her aura.

Zeke, in a surprising move, steps in front of me. "Stay back, bitch." The athame reappears in his hand.

Lyria is my girlfriend. I shouldn't allow Zeke to speak to her in that manner, but I don't say a word. The closer she gets to us, the warier I become. I take a deep breath and catch every single smell in the near vicinity, but what I can't sense is Lyria's wolf scent.

She laughs derisively. "And you plan to stop me with that puny weapon of yours?"

"You're not Lyria," I growl.

She turns her attention to me, then tsks before she morphs into another person, a woman with long red hair and eyes cruel and cold.

"No, but I thought it would be fun to seduce you while wearing the form of the shifter who betrayed your pack."

"What?" I raise my voice.

"Lyria was a two-faced bitch who sold you out to the Shadow Creek pack. Red, your mate, killed her," Zeke supplies. "You can't remember a thing because that motherfucker over there messed with your head."

*Red.* That name stirs something in my chest, a longing that's almost painful.

"I don't know why you're immune to my powers, vermin," she tells Zeke, "but this is the last time you'll get in my way." She pulls her arm back, and a fire spear forms in her hand.

*Holy shit. What the hell is she?*

Zeke acts fast and tosses his weapon in her direction. It

pierces the woman straight in her chest. She lets out an enraged scream while staring at the hilt of the weapon stuck to her body. Her fire spear fizzles into nothing. Lifting her deranged eyes to Zeke, she asks, "How?"

"Oh, that puny weapon of mine? It was made with one of the sacred power stones, bitch. So that means bye-bye." Zeke wiggles his fingers a second before the woman explodes into ashes.

"What the fuck! Did you kill her?" I ask.

Zeke snorts. "I wish. Megaera is one of the Furies. I think only Zeus can kill her, but it's unlikely he will."

I blink fast while my brain tries to process what Zeke just told me. "Come again? Are you talking about Greek mythology here?"

"No, we're discussing Chinese legends." Zeke gives me a droll stare. "Now, come on. I don't know how long it'll take for Megaera to recover her form and return to Crimson Hollow." Zeke heads toward the beginning of the alley.

"Where are we going?" I follow after him.

"We need to get your brothers and then find Red."

Once again the pain fills my heart. Damn. Is what Zeke said true, then? "Is Red really my mate?"

"Yes."

"Why would a Fury make me forget my mate? What did I do to piss off a Greek deity?"

"You didn't do anything. Artemis did."

Zeke veers straight to his business vehicle, a van painted in all colors of the rainbow, which is parked right in front of Hell's Hole. I can't believe I missed it.

It's not until we're both inside and Zeke puts the car in Reverse that I continue. "You need to start telling me the whole story from the beginning."

Zeke throws a pitiful look in my direction and then sighs. "Fine. Here I go again. Let's hope we avoid another reset."

"Come again?"

"This the second time the Furies rearranged your memories. And if I'm to guess, every time they do so, it'll be a worse scenario."

I rub my face and look out the window. "I knew something was off."

"I think that's what the Furies weren't counting on. No matter how many different memories they give you, they can't make you forget your mate completely."

"Does their spell only affect me?"

"Oh no. It affected the entire town."

"Then how come you remember?" I watch the imp intensely.

"Beats me. It also didn't affect Kenya—oh shit. I have to check on her."

"Why?"

"Because the last time I saw her, Tisy turned her into a miniature figurine."

Cursing under my breath, I run a hand through my hair. "Are you sure this isn't a nightmare?"

"Dude, I wish it was."

From the corner of my eye, I catch a brown wolf running toward the road. It's coming fast without any indication that it's going to slow down. "Zeke, watch out!"

He presses on the brakes and the van screeches to a halt. The brown wolf zaps through in front of the vehicle, missing getting hit by it thanks to a miracle.

But another wolf was following him.

Son of a bitch. It's Sam in wolf form. The idiot simply stops on the road right in the vehicle's path and stands there, almost begging to be turned into road pizza.

"What the hell!" Zeke yells.

"It's Sam." I reach for the door handle.

"I know it's him. What's up with your brothers attempting suicide by Zeke Mobile?"

Zeke's comment flies right over my head. But it doesn't matter. I'm out of the car in a flash, and when I get a whiff of Sam's scent in the air, I catch the smell of blood as well. Moving closer, I see his pelt is covered in it.

It's not his blood though, which begs the question: Whose blood is it?

## 13

## SAMUEL

SOMEONE LETS OUT A HOWL AND JARS ME BACK TO THE HERE AND now. At least that's what it feels like. I look around my living room, which is filled with random people, most of them strangers. When did I decide to invite half the bar back to my place? My head is pounding, and I'm a little dizzy. There's a beer bottle in my hand, and I'm sandwiched between two couples making out. Jared is sticking his tongue so far inside his chick's mouth that I'm afraid he'll end up swallowing her tonsils.

I bring the bottle to my lips, but it's fucking empty. Great. I stand on unsteady legs and amble toward the kitchen. Behind the counter, I find Billy, the pack's omega, doing Jell-O shots with a group of girls. *What the hell!* He's only nineteen, and we have a strict rule to abide by human laws. Before I can say anything, he tosses another shot down his throat, throws his hand up in the air, and howls again.

"Billy, what the fuck do you think you're doing?" I ask.

The kid looks at me with glassy red eyes. Son of a bitch. He's toast.

"What? This is a party, isn't it?"

"Apparently, but what are you doing here?"

His eyebrows shoot up to the heavens. "You invited me."

An arm gets tossed around my shoulders, and Armand leans closer. "Loosen up a little, Sammy. The party was your idea."

"I don't remember inviting anyone," I grumble while my head throbs. Shit, the evening isn't even over yet and I'm already hungover.

"I don't think it was his idea." Leo appears to my right with a glass of water in his hand.

"Whose idea was it, then?" I ask.

"Hers." He points at a gorgeous young thing wearing a tight leather dress that leaves nothing to the imagination. Her hair is white blonde and cascades down her back in luscious waves.

Damn, now I understand the poor judgment on my part. She's just the type of woman I'd bend backward to impress. Interestingly enough, looking at her does nothing for my libido. Not even a stir in my pants. It must be the alcohol.

Perhaps sensing my stare, she turns to me. Her eyes are a peculiar light gray, but it's not that detail that gives me goose bumps—and not the good kind. Her eyes are empty, soulless.

"I don't like her," Leo announces.

"You don't like any of the girls I pick up at bars," I say just to be contradictory. He's right about her though. What was I thinking?

"True, but if this"—Leo gestures wildly toward the scene —"isn't proof enough that you have the worst taste in women, I don't know what is."

"Ah, loosen up, Leo. Shake that fox tail of yours." Armand laughs.

"Bite me," he retorts.

"Don't tease me. Speaking of biting shit, I'm hungry." Armand drops his arm from my shoulders and sweeps the room. "So many tasty treats."

He's a half vampire, the only bloodsucker who lives in Crimson Hollow. He jokes all the time about snacking on people, but he doesn't really drink from humans. We wouldn't be friends if he did. But for the first time ever since I met him, I'm sensing the predator in him as he scopes out the crowd. I grab his arm, ready to take him someplace quiet to have a word, when Billy lets out a loud curse and I smell blood in the air.

Armand tenses immediately, his nostrils flaring as he trains his eyes on Billy, who's now covered in vampire dinner. Somehow, the stupid kid found one of Armand's blood bags in the fridge and managed to get it all over him. Faster than lightning, Armand breaks free from my hold and jumps on the omega with fangs bared, sending both of them to the ground.

Panic spreads. The humans scream and run for the door while the supernaturals simply get out of the way and watch the chaos. Jared and Leo immediately jump in to try to dislodge Armand from Billy. I'm about to do the same when I sense a malevolent energy to my left. I turn and find the blonde woman smiling wickedly at the scene. Somehow, I know she's responsible for it.

A wolf's snarl forces me to look away from her. Billy has shifted and is going berserk on Armand's ass. Fuck. If I don't stop them, someone will get seriously hurt.

There's only one way I can make Billy stop. I have to shift. It takes only a few seconds before the sound of my bones cracking mixes with the tearing of my clothes.

*Damn. There goes my favorite leather jacket.*

Jared and Leo have finally managed to drag Armand away from Billy. He thrashes violently against their hold, but it's Billy who I need to control now.

*"Billy! Stop."* I blast the command telepathically.

The smaller wolf is still growling in Armand's direction, and for whatever reason, he's not listening to me. Instead, he advances fast, ready to jump on my friends.

For fuck's sake. I have no choice.

I block the kid by hitting him on the side. He slides across the kitchen floor thanks to the blood he spilled all over it. He smashes against the far wall with a whine but jumps back onto his paws quickly and shakes his head.

Growling and with the fur on his back standing on end, he glances over my head. Hell and damn. He's still riding on the rage of a provoked wolf. I stand in front of him, projecting my alpha stance to the max. From behind, the sounds of struggle tell me Jared and Leo are still having trouble controlling Armand, but I can't worry about them now. Billy should be yielding to me. I'm his alpha, even if I don't exert my position very often.

*"Billy, for the last time, chill the fuck out,"* I say to his mind, but I'm not sure he's even hearing me.

A wicked laugh sounds to my left. It's that damn woman I picked up at the bar. "Poor Samuel. Can't even control his own wolves." She stops next to Billy and touches his head without fear. "Go on, my darling. I command you to challenge your alpha."

Billy's eyes glow yellow before he charges. I attempt to avoid his frontal attack, but I slip on the wet floor. He manages to get a bite on my shoulder, drawing blood. Pure instinct takes over. I'm bigger and stronger than he is. With him still attached to me, I jump to the side, shoving Billy against the cabinet door. He releases his grip on me and falls on his back, exposing his neck. My wolf wants to pin him down and slash his throat. It's what nature demands. But I know this isn't his doing.

My internal debate costs me. Billy slips out from under me and bolts out the door, which is wide open. I don't need to guess who did the favor.

I spare one final glimpse at my roommates. Jared and Leo have somehow rendered Armand unconscious.

"We got this. Go after Billy," Jared urges.

The blonde woman has vanished. How convenient.

I spring after the kid, having no trouble knowing which

direction he went. I'm glad it's snowing tonight and the streets are deserted. We're surrounded by forest, but the sight of two wolves running down the streets of Crimson Hollow would for sure freak out the human folks.

It doesn't take long for me to catch up with Billy. He dashes across the street at the same time headlights illuminate the pavement. I stop running, sensing Tristan is in that car. A moronic thing to do since the vehicle is coming fast. It screeches to a halt just a few inches from me. Damn. I wonder if that fucking woman is nearby, controlling my actions like she did with Billy.

Tristan jumps out of the car, quickly glancing at me before looking into the distance. He curses a moment later.

"What is it?" Zeke Rogers, Crimson Hollow's very own Hell spawn, joins Tristan.

"It's Billy. Something's wrong. I have to shift and go after him."

Fuck. I have to shift back to two legs and tell Tristan what's going on.

"Can't you just howl or something? We don't have time for you to chase after one of your crazy wolves," Zeke retorts.

I return to human form, and immediately the freezing cold makes me curse winter. Hugging myself to keep warm, I approach Tristan and Zeke. "Billy is under some kind of spell. He won't listen to me." Tristan peels off his jacket and drapes it over my shoulder. "Thank you."

"It must have been one of the Furies," Zeke mutters.

"What's going on?" I ask.

"I'll explain in the car. We have to get out of here," he replies.

"We can't simply leave Billy behind. He's not himself. What if he attacks someone?" I argue. Tristan clenches his jaw tight and glances at me. "What? You're siding with the imp? You can't be serious."

He opens his mouth, but a gust of wind comes out of

nowhere, sending snow flurries all around us in a circular motion.

"Fuck! They're coming." Zeke looks at the sky.

The streetlights flicker and a strange energy crackles in the air. Then sudden light appears in the distance, becoming brighter as it approaches us. It descends and the brightness dims, revealing a winged horse wearing golden armor. Lying across the horse's back is Billy, no longer a wolf but most definitely knocked out. He's fully clothed too.

"What the hell," I say.

"Pegasus. Thank fuck. I was beginning to think the Furies had gotten rid of you for good," Zeke says.

"They wouldn't dare. I'm Zeus's champion after all," the horse replies.

Tristan and I trade a glance. The damn horse just spoke. Now I've seen it all.

"What did you do to the wolf pup?" the imp continues.

"He was under Alecto's compulsion. I had no choice but to knock him out. He'll be okay."

Shivering already, I ask, "So you're Pegasus, the mythical Greek creature."

"Yes. We've been through this before," the horse replies with a hint of impatience.

"They got their minds scrubbed again," Zeke explains. "Why aren't you shifting into your warrior form?"

"Zeus is most displeased that I interfered in your affairs. He forbade me from helping."

"And here you are. Don't like to follow rules much, huh?" I smirk.

"Don't be absurd. I'm only here because Zeus allowed. But I can only assist this one time. I'm sorry."

"And how do you plan to help us?" Tristan asks, crossing his arms.

The streetlights begin to flicker again, and the wind picks up once more. Only this time, I know something wicked is coming our way.

"Okay, this is definitely them." Zeke pulls a short sword with a shiny crystal embedded on its hilt out of thin air.

Pegasus trots toward us. "Quickly now, touch my wings."

Zeke immediately does so, but Tristan and I hesitate. The imp glowers at us. "What are you waiting for? Touch the damn wings!"

A cold shiver runs down my spine, announcing the arrival of something very powerful and malevolent. Shit. I don't want to stay and face the newcomer.

Tristan and I both touch the mythical winged horse at once, and bright light envelopes us all. The ground vanishes and my body feels boneless, as light as a feather. The sensation only lasts a few seconds before we drop from a great height, landing awkwardly on a hard surface.

I blink my eyes open while I try to catch my breath. A grunt to my right catches my attention. I sit up and catch Tristan doing the same. Not too far from us are Zeke and Billy, who's slowly coming to. But there's no sign of Pegasus.

"Where are we?" I ask.

Zeke looks around and lets out a string of curses. "Fuck a duck. I can't believe I'm back here."

"Where is here?" Tristan grits out.

"The Wastelands."

14

RED

Nina and I walk side by side down a narrow alleyway that skirts the big market I saw from afar. She seems to know where she's going, but the feeling of doom won't leave my chest. I bring my too-small jacket close together, trying to ward off the chills running through my body.

"So, you don't remember anything at all?" she asks.

"I have memories, but I'm afraid they've been tampered with by the Furies."

"Just when you think you're done dealing with asshole deities, Artemis's past comes to bite you in the ass."

"I don't understand why she won't help us."

"Because she's a jealous bitch."

"Great." I kick a loose pebble, frustrated with everything. "Do you know the way out of this place?"

"Yes. One doesn't come to the Wastelands voluntarily without having an escape route. However, it's not safe in your condition."

"So where are you taking me?"

"To see an old *friend*."

The manner in which she emphasized the word friend clues

me in that this person is anything but. I'm not even sure if I can trust Nina, but it's not like I have any other choice. This memory-loss deal blows.

I tap the breast pocket on my jacket to make sure Kenya is still there. I wish she was here. She'd better be okay once I break the spell those bitches cast on her.

Nina and I reach the end of the alleyway, coming to a vast, barren field that stretches for miles. There's nothing in sight.

"I was really hoping we wouldn't have to venture out in the desert again," I say.

"We aren't." Nina pulls a metallic dial with odd markings around it from inside her jacket. At its center is a yellow, multifaceted stone that seems to pulse from within.

"What's that?"

"The key to the back door of the palace." She smirks before raising the medallion.

There's a ripple around the strange object, almost as if Nina touched water. The ripple is quickly followed by sparks of electricity. In an instant, a wooden door materializes out of thin air. The stone is now embedded in the surface. Letting go of the object, Nina pushes the door open and crosses into the unknown.

"Come on, Red," she calls from within.

A shiver of apprehension runs down my spine as I follow her, and my jaw drops of its own accord when I take in the room. The magical door led to a wide hallway that, thanks to its décor, I can only assume belongs to a castle. The ceiling must be at least twenty feet high. To my left, tall windows let through sunshine, and the colored glass details on top create a prism effect where the light hits.

"Amazing. But there's no sun outside."

"No. What you see here is nothing but an illusion. Come on. We must speak with Prythian at once."

I furrow my brows. That name sounds familiar, but as hard

as I try to remember who it belongs to, I can't. All I get is an uncomfortable itch in my brain, one I can't scratch.

Fuck the Furies.

Nina strides ahead with the confidence of one who knows what they're doing. I quicken my pace to keep up with her, not wanting to get lost in this place. She stops in front a set of double doors at the end of the hallway. They're manned on each side by tall sentries dressed in full knight regalia. They're too bulky and wide to be human.

"You again. What do you want, fox?" the guard on the left asks.

"Hello, Tweedle Dum. I'm here to speak with your boss."

The guard grunts. "He's busy."

"Doing what? Changing his hair color for the umpteenth time?"

The ground and walls shake, rattling the oil paints hanging from them. *Who the hell is doing that?* The guards trade a glance, and then the one on the right shrugs.

"Let them through. If the King of Bastards decides to obliterate them, it's not our concern."

Grumbling, his companion pushes one of the doors open. "Go in already."

*King of Bastards?* I don't like the sound of that at all. But Nina walks in without hesitation, so I follow close behind.

If I thought the hallway was impressive, I don't have words to describe the room I'm currently in now. There's gold everywhere, plus impressive classical art that would put envy in the hearts of any museum curator. I honestly don't know what to gawk at first.

That thought flies right out of my head when I catch movement in my peripheral vision, followed by an immeasurable source of power. Slowly, I turn toward it, finding a tall, beautiful man with long jet-black hair and cunning, hard eyes staring at me. He's not human, that much I can gauge.

"What the hell are you doing back here, Nina? You were supposed to be on a job."

"As you can see, I came across a peculiar situation." She glances at me.

The ethereal man moves closer. He doesn't make a sound as he walks. It's almost as if he's gliding. I curl my hands protectively over my belly and take a step backward. The malice he's projecting is giving me goose bumps and making me wish Nina never brought me here.

"Red, I didn't think I'd ever see you again in my domain." His gaze drops to my protruding belly. "And in that condition to boot."

"Have we met?" I croak.

He raises an eyebrow and then turns his attention to Nina. "What's going on?"

"She doesn't remember you or ever coming here."

The male wrinkles his forehead and looks back at me. "Interesting."

Shivers run down my spine as I endure his malicious and cunning stare.

"Hey! Don't you be having any ideas about Red. Remember our deal," Nine says.

His lips become nothing but a thin, flat line as he narrows his eyes. "I didn't forget our deal, fox spy. But the fact that you brought the wolf shifter here makes me believe that perhaps you have."

"I didn't forget anything. But I couldn't abandon her in the Wastelands desert. She's my friend."

He shakes his head. "For a mercenary, you care too much about others. That won't help you in your quest."

Nina glowers at the male but doesn't offer a retort. I have no idea what they're talking about, but it's not about me or how to get me out of here, so I open my mouth to speak up.

"Nina said you could help me."

The King of Bastards walks leisurely toward a liquor tray and pours wine into a crystal chalice before he replies, "I suppose Nina didn't tell you how hard it is to leave the Wastelands. I can help you, but it'll require payment."

"What kind of payment?" I grit out.

He brings the chalice to his lips and watches me through the rim.

"Add helping Red to my tab," Nina says before the King of Bastards can reply.

His brows arch as he stares at her. "Your tab is already a mile long."

She shrugs. "Exactly. One more favor won't change much."

I shouldn't accept Nina's offer, but I can't make a deal with the male blindly. Plus, I have to think about my babies too.

"I'll think about it," he replies.

It makes my blood boil. Curling my hands into fists, I state, "There's no time for you ponder shit. I can't remain trapped here. I have to get back to my mates and find a way to defeat the Furies."

His eyebrows shoot to the heavens. "The Furies are after you?" He whistles. "I don't envy you."

I feel a kick, which reminds me that I haven't peed in like twenty minutes, which means I'm due again.

"Thanks for that useful remark. Where's your bathroom?"

The powerful male keeps staring at me without blinking, as if what I just asked is a puzzle or something.

"Hello?" I wave my hand.

"Give him a second, Red. Prythian is still trying to process such a mundane question. He's not used to the banalities of common living," Nina replies.

"Well, if he doesn't answer fast, I'll pee right here all over his Persian rug."

"There's no need for such a barbaric act." He flicks his hand, and in an instant, the urge to pee vanishes.

I let out a gasp, covering my belly. "What did you do to me?"

"I took care of your problem. Now, you were say—" He stops suddenly and clenches his jaw. As if he's listening to something, he cocks his head to the side. After a moment, he continues. "You don't need to worry about getting to your mates anymore."

"What's that supposed to mean?" I take a step forward, my heart beating at a staccato rhythm now.

"They're here."

---

DANTE

I should shift to my wolf, but I don't think I'll have enough time to do so. Instead, I raise both hands and shuffle backward slowly, not taking my eyes off the monster hissing at me. It reminds me of a monitor lizard, if the large reptile had two heads and glowing red eyes.

My eyes drop to its developed limbs. I bet it can outrun me while I'm in human form. From the corner of my eye, I try to find anything I can use as weapon. But there's nothing for miles besides a gray, dry land. There's only one alternative, break into a run and shift during it.

I prepare to bolt when I hear the echo of someone cursing down the canyon a few yards from me. The creature's attention also diverts to the noise. Now it's my chance to get a head start, but when a familiar voice reaches me, I freeze.

It's Tristan.

*What the hell is he doing here?*

The lizard monster turns its snout up and flares its nostrils. Then he returns to his kill, ignoring me completely—at least for now. I inch toward the edge of the canyon without taking my eyes off the creature, but when I reach the crevice, I peel my eyes off it to glance down. Tristan, Sam, Billy, and Zeke are down below. Since neither of my brothers is in wolf form, I can't reach them telepathically. I stick my index finger and thumb in my mouth and whistle loudly.

They all look up.

"Dante? What are you doing here?" Sam asks, and his voice carries loudly.

"Shut up, you idiot. You're not in Kansas anymore," Zeke retorts in a much lower tone, but down in the canyon, every sound gets amplified.

Behind me, the devilish lizard hisses again. I look over my shoulder and find the creature staring in the opposite direction. There's a small hill but nothing out of the ordinary until a cold breeze picks up, bringing to my nose the foul stench of rotten meat. Fuck, something nasty is coming.

I turn to the guys, who are now attempting to climb out of the canyon on my side. I wave maniacally to make them stop, but none are looking in my direction. For fuck's sake. I bend over and pick up a small piece of rock. I throw it in Zeke's direction, since he's the one leading the ascension. The rock hits the ground right in front of the imp, making too much noise for my liking.

Zeke looks up, mouth open to say something, when I signal for him to be quiet. Then I try to find the best path to go down the ravine and get out of sight.

Skittering behind me makes me turn. With a piece of raw meat in his large jaws, the monster lizard runs past me and hurries down the canyon. It doesn't take long for me to understand why. A horde of tall creatures appears on top of the hill, all carrying wicked-looking weapons. They wear rudimentary armor and fur, and their skins are different shades of gray and green. With their large noses and tusks protruding from inside their mouths, they can only be one thing—trolls.

With a battle cry, they raise their swords, spears, and axes and charge down the hill.

*Son of a bitch.* The time to be cautious is over.

I head down, following the path of dust the lizard left in its wake.

"What was that?" Billy asks, already back at the bottom of the canyon with the others.

Halfway down, I lose my footing on a loose rock, and the momentum sends me tumbling down the rest of the way. I hit my elbows and shoulders several times as I try to protect my head from banging against the hard surface.

My skull is throbbing, but I don't miss the guttural sounds of the approaching horde. The soft thud of someone landing next to me catches my attention.

With a brusque movement, Tristan yanks me from the ground.

"Come on! We have to find cover."

We run across the canyon without a clear destination in mind. There's nowhere to hide, so our only hope of escaping is to reach the other side and climb out.

"Should we shift?" Billy asks.

"And leave me behind? You know I can't run as fast as you in wolf form," Zeke complains.

"Tough shit," Sam replies.

"You're an ungrateful son of a bitch. I'm in this situation because I was trying to help you, jackass."

"We're not shifting," Tristan grunts.

We reach the other side of the canyon, and I finally dare to look over my shoulder. The trolls have descended en masse and are fast approaching, perched on their grotesque mounts.

"We gotta climb up fast." I reach for the rocky wall, testing the protruding formation before putting my weight on it, when a spear flies an inch from my ear and pierces the spot next to my hand. "Fuck! That was close."

"They're coming!" Billy shouts.

I whirl on the spot, fangs and claws already on display. We

don't have a choice but to shift and fight the approaching trolls. We're sorely outnumbered. There are at least twenty of them, heavily armed, and that's without counting their mounts. We'll be shredded in less than a minute.

Suddenly, the sound of a horn echoes in the valley. It's coming from above us. The horde slows until they stop completely. All trolls have their gazes upward.

"Shit. Someone else is coming," Zeke mutters.

"Look, the trolls seem uneasy now. That's good, right?" Billy points out.

"It depends. If they're afraid, then the new party is much more dangerous than they are."

The horn sounds again before the troll leading the horde is skewered by a lance. He spits dark blood from his mouth and falls from his hideous steed. His companions stare at him for a couple of seconds before retreating as fast as they can.

I turn around and look up. A tall man with long black hair sits proudly atop a russet warhorse. There's no sun here, but his black armor seems to shine nonetheless. He stares straight at me, and then recognition hits me.

It's Prythian, the King of Bastards.

## 15

RED

"THIS IS MADNESS. WHY WOULDN'T PRYTHIAN LET US GO WITH him?" I ask.

"How many times are you going to ask me that?" Nina replies from her prone position on the white chaise lounge.

"Ugh! How can you be so calm about it? He's evil. Do you trust him?"

Nina snorts. "Prythian? Not even as far as I can throw him." She throws her legs off the couch and leans forward, resting her elbows on her knees. "He's not called the King of Bastards for no reason. He's a banished high fae lord from one of the Unseelie Kingdoms."

"Are you talking Unseelie and Seelie courts here?"

"Yeah, but unlike the legends you've probably heard, there's more than one wicked court in Faerie land."

"How do you know so much about the fae?"

Nina's expression becomes a cold mask. "I'm a spy. It's my business to know everything about everyone."

Her logic is sound, but I sense Nina's interest in the fae is personal. I'm not sure why I'm getting this strange feeling when I don't even remember meeting her to begin with.

A prickly sensation on the back of my neck makes the small hairs stand on end. I whirl on the spot and face the double doors. My heart begins to beat faster, and the yearning there is overwhelming.

My mates are here.

As if sensing their fathers' approach, I feel the babies move and kick.

The doors to Prythian's lavish room open and in comes the dark fae lord. His hair, which was jet black before he left, is now a light gray. But it's his solemn expression that gives me pause. I'm about to ask him what happened when Tristan, Samuel, and Dante follow the fae male.

I take a step forward and then stop abruptly. My heart skips a beat as I scan the three wolf shifters' expressions. I see a mix of worry, relief, and anger in their gazes. Samuel is the first to move in my direction, breaching the distance between us in three long strides. He pulls me into his arms, engulfing me in a bear hug. I melt into his embrace, my body recognizing the man even if my brain doesn't.

"You're okay," he murmurs.

"It was close," I reply.

I feel something hard poke my chest—Kenya's figurine. It's a reminder that I must find a way to defeat the Furies and get my best friend back. Reluctantly, I ease out of Samuel's embrace and find Tristan and Dante near us.

"How can it be?" Tristan asks in awe. "I have no memory of you, but I sense the bond."

"It seems that as powerful as the Furies are, they couldn't break the bond between you and Red," Prythian chimes in.

"You should start from there to regain your memories," Zeke says. "The question is how." He rubs his chin and assumes a pensive countenance.

I didn't even notice he was in the room, too riveted on my mates. And he's not alone. A young man stands next to him.

"Billy? What are you doing here?" Nina asks.

He frowns. "Have we met?"

She glances at me with an eyebrow raised. Before she voices her question, Zeke answers, "The memory spell affected the entire town save for me and Kenya Arantes."

"Oh." Nina looks in Billy's direction again with a disappointed expression on her face.

"Prythian, can you undo the Furies' spell?" Dante asks.

His tone of familiarity gives me pause. "Wait. Do you remember him?"

"Yeah, for some reason, I knew who he was."

"Don't sound so surprised, Dante. We shared a lot during your time in my company." I catch the double meaning in the fae's words, which ignites an overwhelming sense of possession.

"What's that supposed to mean?" I practically growl.

"Whoa. Put your claws away, darling." Prythian lifts his hands in a mock gesture of peace. "I was teasing. Dante had a vision about me. It's possible that memory was embedded too deeply for it to be affected by the Furies' spell."

"Didn't he have several visions about Red too?" Nina argues. "But he still can't remember her."

"That's not completely true," Dante replies. "I retained a partial memory of Red, unlike Tristan and Sam."

"That's interesting." Prythian narrows his eyes.

"Interesting meaning you can help us?" I ask eagerly, forgetting for a moment who I'm talking to.

He cocks his head to the side, first staring into my eyes and then at Dante. "No. But I may know a way you can recover your memories without any help from outsiders."

"How?" Tristan asks.

"By ignoring your human logic and letting your animal instinct take over. Your bond is still intact, yeah?"

"I can feel the tug." Tristan glances in my direction, piercing me with his intense gray eyes. "It's the strongest thing I've ever felt in my life."

Heat rushes to my cheeks while my heartbeat takes off at warp speed. "I feel it too."

"That makes sense," Zeke chimes in. "But if you're going to let your animal side loose, I'd suggest doing it soon. When the Furies discover we're all in the Wastelands, they'll be coming for us with everything they've got."

"It'll take a while for them to find this place, but I agree with the imp, don't waste any time. My suggestion might not work after all."

"I still don't know what you mean by letting our animal instincts take over," I say. Everyone's eyes are on me now, making me feel like I said something stupid. "What?"

"I'm going out on a limb here and say he means you need to mate," Nina replies with a straight face.

My jaw drops while my face bursts into flames. But a quick glimpse at the three brothers tells me she wasn't joking. My heart is thundering in my chest now, and my mouth is as dry as a desert. But my crazy hormones are completely on board with the idea of having sex with three men at the same time.

Mortified, I look away. "I don't know if I can do that."

"Did you have to be so blunt in your response?" Zeke addresses Nina.

"What? I thought time was of the essence. No sense in beating around the bush. And she's clearly done it before." She points at my pregnant belly.

"Can I have a moment alone with my... mates, please?" I ask without making eye contact with them.

"Naturally." Prythian smiles, but the glint in his eyes doesn't comfort me. He snaps his fingers before I can say anything, and suddenly I'm no longer in his luxurious chamber but in an equally extravagant suite.

"Son of a bitch. Who is that guy?" Samuel asks.

I whirl on the spot, confirming that Dante and Tristan were also transported to the room with us. I can't deny the raw attraction I'm feeling for them right now. I'm so nervous, shakes run through my body.

"Don't be afraid, Red," Dante says, taking a tentative step toward me.

"I'm not afraid," I reply.

Tristan rubs his face, peeling his eyes away from me for a moment. I follow his gaze, finding the biggest bed I've ever seen in my entire life. It could easily accommodate ten people on it. It's a bed made for group sex, which is what's supposed to happen now.

Oh my God. Someone kill me.

"You're nervous though. Don't be," Samuel pipes up, interrupting my internal freak-out. "To be honest, I'm nervous too."

I snort, an involuntary reaction. "You're saying that Samuel Wolfe, the notorious manwhore of Crimson Hollow, is nervous at the prospect of having a foursome."

He winces as if I'd slapped him, making me regret my harsh words.

"I'm sorry. My tongue gets extra sharp when I'm feeling cornered."

He smiles briefly, showing the hint of a pair of sexy dimples. "Don't apologize. I deserve to be called that."

I drop my gaze to my belly, placing my hands over it. "I'm sure you put your scandalous ways behind you when we bonded."

"The Furies messed with our memories, but they couldn't completely erase the sentiment in my heart. Since this whole nightmare started, every time I looked at another woman, I didn't feel any desire toward her. That's gotta say something."

"It's like what Prythian said. The Furies gave us new memories, but they couldn't trick our wolf essence. It remembers." Dante pierces me with his smoldering green eyes.

Swallowing the huge lump in my throat, I ask, "Do you think that if we shifted into our wolf forms, we could break the spell?"

"Probably, but you can't shift while you're that far in your pregnancy. It's not safe," Tristan replies.

"So the only solution is...." I can't finish that sentence, nor withstand their gazes, so I drop my eyes to the floor.

I sense them moving closer, and with their approach, the yearning increases. My very bones are on fire now. I suck in a breath when Samuel circles behind me and touches my arms.

"It's okay, Red. Relax," he whispers in my ear.

"I'm trying, but this is so hard."

Dante stops in front of me. "I know it is. But you can trust us."

I peer into his eyes, finding nothing but sincerity and compassion there.

"What should I do?"

"Close your eyes and feel the wolf's energy swirling in your chest. Let it guide you."

I look over Dante's shoulder, locking gazes with Tristan. Out of the three brothers, he's the most serious one, even a little scary. But I become less nervous as I get lost in his steady gaze.

"You can do it, Red," he says.

With a shaky breath, I close my eyes, focusing on the wild essence I feel in the middle of my chest. I wince when I'm blasted by my wolf's torment. She remembers her mates, and she's crying for them. Instinctively, I know she wants to break free, which I can't allow.

*What if I lose control and end up shifting by accident? Tristan said it's dangerous for me right now. What if I end up hurting my babies?*

"It's okay, Red. You're not going to lose control," Dante says softly.

My eyes fly open. "How did you hear me? Did I say that out loud?"

Dante's expression becomes guilty. "I'm sorry. I didn't mean to read your thoughts, but you were projecting them pretty loud. I couldn't block them fast enough."

"Are you saying you can read minds?" I squeak.

"In wolf form, we have the ability to connect telepathically. Dante is the only one who can communicate with us while human."

I step away from them, veering for the bed. Taking a seat at the edge, I attempt to control my nerves. "That's a lot to take in at once."

Samuel follows me to the bed and drops into a crouch in front of me. "We're bonded mates. We'll go through it together." His hand hovers over my knee. "May I?"

"Yeah."

The moment his warm hand touches me, an incendiary flame ignites in the pit of my stomach. My breathing becomes shallow, and I can almost hear my wolf howling inside.

"Damn. We *are* mated. My wolf is going crazy," Samuel says.

"Mine too," I breathe.

"Can I kiss you?" he asks.

My lips part of their own accord. I want to say yes, but my human convictions hold me back. I look at Tristan and Dante, who are watching the scene with matching smoldering gazes. They're unbothered by Samuel's proximity to me. How is that possible?

"Go ahead, Red. Kiss him if you want to," Tristan replies.

I switch my attention to Samuel, not daring to breathe. Boldly, I cup his cheek, loving the feel of his scruff against my hand. He runs his fingers up my arms, and despite the layers of fabric, I can feel the heat from his touch just the same. Overcome by a raw need to taste him, I lean down and kiss his sinful mouth. He lets me explore, but I sense it's taking every ounce of willpower on his part to let me set the pace.

But soon, not even I'm in control anymore. The wolf takes over, and what was a slow and probing kiss becomes wild and fiery. Samuel grabs my face between his hands and deepens the kiss. I hear growls in the background as the scent of arousal spreads everywhere. I'm too hot, and my clothes are suddenly too confining.

With difficulty, I ease back, breaking the kiss. Samuel's eyes are now glowing wolfish yellow.

"What is it, sweetheart?" he asks.

I glance at Dante and Tristan, who somehow haven't moved an inch. "I need help getting out of my clothes."

Samuel looks over his shoulder. "Are you just going to stand there? You heard her."

"Is that okay, Red?" Tristan asks.

"Y-Yes."

He and Dante come to the bed and awkwardly help me out of my jacket. I tense, despite wanting this to happen. I'm not sure if the block is coming from my human head or if the Furies are somehow responsible for my hesitation too.

My mates sense the change in my demeanor and stop.

"We don't need to continue," Dante says in a voice that's so loaded with need, it sends shivers down my spine.

"Yes we do. Kiss me." I reach for the back of his head and pull him to me before I lose my nerve.

When his tongue touches mine, I melt in his arms. I also feel the last tendrils of resistance snap. The wolf's wild essence fills my head, spurring me on. I break the kiss with Dante and turn to Tristan, who's on my left side. Samuel is still crouched in front of me, rubbing my thighs up and down. With each trip, his hands get closer to my hips.

Dante kisses my shoulder while his fingers trace down my arm, brushing the underside of my breast. Arching my back, I grab his hand and place it over my boob. Without missing a beat, he begins to toy with it, squeezing and rubbing his thumb over my nipple.

"Fuck, baby. I want to kiss you right here." Samuel slides his fingers across my pelvis, making my clit throb in anticipation.

Tristan lets go of my lips with a soft pop before turning his attention to my neck.

Breathlessly, I tell Samuel, "Go ahead."

He pulls my leggings and panties down slowly, making me feel a tad self-conscious. But those pesky thoughts are completely erased from my mind when he parts my legs and sweeps his tongue across my clit.

"Oh my God," I cry out.

"You can say that again. You taste divine, baby," he murmurs, blowing hot breath against my feverish skin.

I close my eyes and succumb to the pleasure my mates are giving me. There's a tug, and then my top is off. Two hot mouths latch on each of my breasts—Tristan's and Dante's—to tease me beyond sanity while Samuel's tongue does its magic between my legs.

Pleasure keeps building and building, spreading throughout my entire body. I don't know where I end and they begin. I grab a handful of Samuel's hair and yank it hard. In response, he inserts two fingers inside of me and begins to pump in and out in sync with the pace of his tongue.

"I can't hold it any longer," I say.

Growls are what I get as replies. A moment later, the most intense orgasm hits me, wreaking havoc on my body. It seems to go on forever and yet not long enough.

Suddenly, flashes of my life with my mates appear before my eyes. The first time I saw them when I had just turned into a wolf, all the sweet moments we shared as bonded wolves, the fight against the archdemon Harkon, me going after Dante and Sam when Artemis took them.

I remember *everything*.

# 16

## RED

I'M BONELESS, MY BODY STILL TREMBLING FROM MY RELEASE, BUT my brain is as sharp as ever. With a gasp, I open my eyes. Tristan, Dante, and Sam are no longer kissing me. Instead, the three of them are staring wide-eyed at me.

"Red? Do you remember us?" Sam asks.

I'm swept up by emotion, so the only thing I can do is nod.

Tristan and Dante hug me from each side, making a sandwich out of me.

"Thank goodness, my love," Dante chokes out.

"I can't believe we didn't remember you," Tristan adds. "I'm so fucking mad at myself."

"Don't be. The Furies are powerful deities. We didn't stand a chance."

"Still, I should be able to see through their bullshit." He captures my face in his hand, forcing me to look into his eyes. "You're my mate, Red. No one should have the power to make me forget you."

"Our wolves didn't forget," I say.

"Thank fuck for that." Sam places a hand over my belly. "How are the babies? Are they okay?"

"I think so. Aside from some kicks here and there, I have no complaints."

Tristan jumps out of bed, his body coiled with tension. "I'm going to kill those bitches!"

"There's one for each of us," Sam pipes up.

"Hey! What about me? They messed with my family," I whine.

Tristan furrows his brow. "You can have Artemis. She refused to help, after all."

"No one is going after any deity without a plan." Dante gets up from the bed, and my eyes drop to his massive erection.

Tristan is still obviously aroused too, and I don't need to glance at Sam's crotch to know he's also sporting a boner. Suddenly, the need for retaliation gets pushed to the back of my mind. My pussy clenches as if begging me to finish what we started.

Tristan and Dante both turn to me at once, probably sensing my arousal.

"Before we rush into danger, can we… continue?" I ask.

Their eyes flash again, turning ember, a sign of undiluted desire. I scooch back on the massive bed to make room for them. At once, my mates join me, their mouths and hands touching every inch of my body. Knowing we're on borrowed time, we don't waste time with more foreplay. I'm wet and ready, and so are they.

With my belly in the way, there aren't many positions we can attempt, so I opt for the one we've been favoring for the past month. I get on my knees, offering my pussy to whoever is clos-est. Dante grabs me by the hips and with a swift move, he plunges inside of me. I cry out, but soon making noises becomes a problem. Tristan is kneeling in front of me in all his naked glory. Licking my lips, I look up, and then I wrap my fingers around his cock. With a wicked smile, I kiss the sensitive head first, teasing him with my tongue. He hisses and grabs a handful of my hair.

"God, I love when you suck me." He takes charge and fucks my mouth.

"And when you use your hand," Sam says to my right.

Bracing one hand against the mattress, I search for Sam with my other. He moves, kneeling within my reach. I take his cock and begin to pump up and down his length. Our lovemaking becomes a beautiful orchestra of moans, grunts, and murmurs. Nothing else matters besides giving and receiving caresses. Time ceases to exist, but when another powerful wave of pleasure sweeps over me, I know our session wasn't long enough.

We yell at the same time, climaxing in unison. Once again, my legs turn into mush, and as soon as Dante slips out, I collapse on the mattress sideways. A second later, three pairs of arms wrap around me, Tristan and Sam on each of my sides and Dante hugging my legs.

"This was amazing," I say.

"Best one yet," Sam agrees.

"Too bad we're not home," Tristan adds.

"We need to get going," Dante replies.

"True," I say, but I don't move and neither do they.

I close my eyes for a second with every intention of getting up in five minutes or so. That doesn't happen. Somehow, we've all fallen asleep, and when I wake up, I sense we're no longer alone in the room. A throat clearing tells me I'm right.

Unable to move thanks to my mates, I do the only thing I can.

I yell.

Tristan, Dante, and Sam sit up at once as if they'd been electrocuted.

"Relax, it's just me."

Prythian appears suddenly, sitting leisurely on a chair in the corner of the room.

"What the hell! How long have you been here?" I try to cover my naked body with my arms, but my mates are now standing at the foot of the bed, creating a protective barrier.

"Were you spying on us, you perv?" Tristan growls.

"Please. Don't flatter yourself. You were taking too long, so I came to investigate. Your friends were fretting and getting on my nerves."

"We fell asleep." I scooch out of bed and look for my clothes.

Sam turns around and gathers everything before I can. "Here, my love."

"My love?" Prythian asks. "Does that mean you've broken the Furies' spell?"

"Yes. Now can we have some privacy?" Dante replies.

"Oh, please. Since when are shifters modest?"

"Since you're in the room," Sam retorts.

He's not wrong, but now that I remember what he did to us the last time we were here, I'm leery of the male. I get dressed as fast as I can, then circle around the guys.

"We need to get back to Crimson Hollow. Are you going to help us or not?"

Prythian cocks his head to the side. "Nina agreed to pay for my assistance, so yes. But you need better clothes, darling."

He snaps his fingers, and bam, my clothes actually fit now.

"Is this an illusion like everything is in this place?" I ask.

"No." He flicks his wrist, and not only do we return to Prythian's receiving room but the guys are all dressed again.

Zeke jumps from his spot on the couch. "Fuck. You almost gave me a heart attack. I hate these instant pop-ins."

"So, did it work?" Nina asks.

"Yes. We got our memories back," I say.

Billy frowns. "Then how come I don't remember anything?"

"You're not part of Red's harem, pup. They were able to break the spell because of their bond. I'm afraid everyone else in

Crimson Hollow will remain clueless until the Furies are defeated."

I gasp, remembering Kenya's figurine, which was in the breast pocket of my old jacket. "What happened to Kenya?"

"Who?" Prythian turns to me.

"My friend. The Furies turned her into a miniature figure. She was in my pocket."

"Ah. You mean this figurine?" The object appears between Prythian's fingers. He tosses it in my direction without a care in the world.

I stretch my arm to catch it before it hits the ground. "What the hell! This is my friend!"

"And right now she's a toy. She won't get hurt." He shrugs.

"What's your game plan once you return to Crimson Hollow?" Nina asks.

"You're not coming with us?" Billy looks at her with eyebrows raised.

"No. I can't."

"We don't have a plan, and that's the problem. Maybe we should stay here longer until we figure out what to do," Zeke suggests.

"I can't just stay here and do nothing," I argue.

"Who let the Furies escape in the first place?" Prythian asks suddenly.

"They were in a prison in the Underworld. That's Hades's domain," Zeke replies, a glint of interest in his eyes.

"So maybe you should pay him a visit," the fae continues.

"Are you crazy? One does not simply walk into the Underworld without proper invitation," Zeke retorts.

"Do you think Pegasus can get us an invitation?" I ask, because going to pay Hades a visit is shaping up to be our best solution right now.

"He's Zeus's champion. I'm sure he could," Zeke replies. "That is, if the Furies haven't barbecued his horsy ass."

"The Furies have messed with our minds twice. What's keeping them from erasing our memories again?" Tristan asks.

Fear spears my chest. I hadn't thought of that possibility.

"I could put a protective barrier in your minds that would prevent them from getting access," Prythian replies.

"Hell to the no. You're not going anywhere near my head," Sam retorts.

"Are you for real, Samuel? Would you rather have some psycho bitch get in there?" Nina puts her hands on her hips and glowers.

"Nina is right. We can't return to Crimson Hollow unprotected. Who knows how long it'll take to contact Pegasus," I say.

"Ugh. Fine." Sam throws his hands up in the air. "I'll let the Bastard King put the barrier in place."

Prythian's hair, which was almost white a moment ago, turns pitch black in the blink of an eye. "It's King of Bastards," he grits out. "And helping you out will require payment."

"Are you for real?" I throw him a death glare. "Can't you do anything for others without asking for something in return?"

"I could, but it's more fun to watch mortals squirm, trying to pay me back." He smiles in a chilling manner.

"I'll bite. What do you want in exchange for your assistance?" Tristan asks.

"Don't even think about asking for my firstborn," I warn him.

Prythian places a hand over his chest and twists his face into a phony offended expression. "I wouldn't dream of asking such atrocious payment. Do you think I'm a heartless monster?"

"Yes," my mates and I answer in unison.

The fae doesn't blink for several beats, but then he drops the mask of innocence. "Fine. You got me there. Truth is, I don't want anything from you." He looks meaningfully in Zeke's direction.

The imp's spine goes rigid in an instant. "What? You want something from *me*?"

"Yes."

"What?"

"A favor."

Squinting, Zeke crosses his arms. "What favor?"

"You'll know when the time comes."

Billy snorts. "That's dumb."

Nina elbows him in the arm and not so subtly urges him to keep his mouth shut. Thankfully, Prythian ignores his retort.

"Look, pal, I wasn't born yesterday. I know all about secret favors and shady contracts. I'm an agent of Hell, after all." Zeke scoffs. "I'm not about to enter into a deal with you without knowing the payment."

Prythian shrugs. "Suit yourself. I can send you folks right back to Crimson Hollow without protection. How long do you think it'll take for the Furies to do another number with your friends' minds?"

I want to beg Zeke to agree, but I can't ask him knowing how foul Prythian can be. I've never met a creature more mercurial than him.

The imp looks in my direction, and I see the turmoil in his gaze. No one speaks for several beats, until finally Zeke turns to Prythian once more.

"Fine. You have yourself a deal."

"You're such a good friend." Prythian smiles.

I let out a relieved breath, but now comes the part where the dark fae has to enter our minds.

Eyes shining with mirth, Prythian moves in my direction. Immediately, my mates block his way.

"You're not starting with Red," Tristan says.

"Silly wolf. Do you think I need to work on you one by one?"

Before anyone can reply, Prythian's magic surrounds us. I

feel a featherlight touch against my forehead, and a second later, the sensation is gone.

"It's done," he announces.

17

---

RED

Prythian sent us back to the compound, but he warned us that the Furies might have changed people's memories again while we were gone. Basically, we don't know what kind of situation we'll find. We lock ourselves in what used to be our room, but in this reality, it's still Tristan's old bedroom. Billy and Zeke tag along, which makes this situation even more awkward.

"We should have tried to convince Nina to come with us," Billy says.

"Wait, do you remember her?" I cock my head to the side, daring to hope he somehow recovered his memories.

"I'm not sure how to answer that question. I know who she is, the fox spy. Are we friends in the real world?"

Zeke snorts, and the guys look at everything but the kid.

"You can say that," I reply.

Billy rubs the back of his neck and glances down. "That would explain why I was drawn to her."

Zeke claps him on the shoulder. "Don't worry, buddy. We just have to figure out a way to defeat some vengeful goddesses and you'll recover all your lovely memories."

I catch the sarcasm in Zeke's tone, but thankfully Billy doesn't. The last year was filled with happy memories, but there were way too many terrible ones too, such as Seth's demise. If I had my way, I'd make sure Billy never recovered the memory of his brother's death.

Unable to keep staring at Billy and worrying about what we have to do, I glance around. A picture frame on Tristan's drawer catches my attention. My stomach clenches painfully at the sight. I know nothing here is real, but the picture of Tristan and Lyria in a lover's embrace is too much to bear. My canines descend, and a low growl erupts from my throat.

Tristan follows my line of sight.

"Shit." He puts the picture frame down. "I'm sorry, love. The Furies thought it would be amusing to resurrect that traitorous bitch."

"I hate them," I say.

"What's going to happen now? How do we find Pegasus?" Billy asks.

We all turn to Zeke.

"How should I know?" he asks.

"You're immune to the Furies' spell," I reply.

"So what? I know nothing about deities. Weren't Sam and Dante Artemis's wolves? Can't they figure it out?"

"When we chose Red, we severed our connection to Artemis," Sam replies.

"Hmm, but Red still bears her mark." Dante turns to me.

"Wait. You want *me* to call that bitch?"

"Not her. Pegasus."

"I wouldn't know where to start."

"You'd better find out fast. We're sitting ducks here. I'm sure the Furies can sense we've returned to Crimson Hollow." Zeke walks to the window and opens the curtains to peer outside. He's definitely on edge, but so am I.

The room begins to shake suddenly. Dante pulls me into his arm and drags me away from the door.

"Fuck, too late. They've found us," Zeke whines.

Billy gets into a defensive stance, but it's no use. They'll end up hurting him like they did Kenya.

"Get out of there, Billy!" I shout.

The door doesn't burst open or explode like I had imagined. Instead, Pegasus materializes in the room in his winged horse form. Too big for the confined space, his wing hits a lamp, sending it crashing to the floor. Billy jumps back, colliding with Tristan, who steadies him.

"What the hell!" Sam yells.

"Sorry about your room, but I'm still forbidden from appearing in my human form," Pegasus explains.

"That's so freaky," Billy murmurs.

"We need your help getting an audience with Hades," I say, not wasting any time.

"What for? He won't help you."

"He was the one who let the Furies escape in the first place. He's our last chance."

A loud crash outside makes me jump on the spot. "That's them, isn't it?"

"Yes."

"Come on, dude. Take us to Hades now!" Sam commands.

"Hades wasn't banished to the Underworld for nothing. He'll be furious if I bring you there."

"He can't be worse than those three bitches," I say.

"Take them already," Zeke interrupts. "Billy and I will distract the Furies."

"Zeke, no—"

"It's okay, Red. If you succeed, we'll be fine."

A loud boom echoes outside, and then the walls begin to crack. Shit. They're going to level the manor.

"If we're going to the Underworld, it has to be now!" Dante shouts over the loud, constant noise.

Pegasus hangs his head. "Very well, but be prepared to deal with Hades's wrath."

Once again, we're surrounded by a vortex of light that lasts no more than a few seconds. When we land on the rough ground, my nose can immediately tell we're in the bowels of the world. The vortex light vanishes to reveal a dark cave with rocks that shimmer crimson. Pegasus is standing in front of us, back into his human form.

"How come you're on two legs here?" Sam asks.

"I'm in a god's domain. My limitations only applied to the human realm."

"Is this where Hades lives? Kind of drab, isn't it?" Sam looks around.

"This is one of the entrances to his hall."

"Wait, no guards? What about that three-headed dog?"

"Cerberus doesn't keep anyone from entering, he prevents people from leaving."

"That's just great," Tristan mumbles.

Pegasus walks ahead. "Please, let me do all the talking."

We walk for about ten minutes before the tunnel widens and we enter a much bigger chamber. It's brighter here, though not lighter. At the end of the room is a dais and a lonely, dark throne with a beautiful man sitting leisurely on it. His legs are spread wide, and he's leaning sideways on one of the arms with a dark chalice in his hand. He has black hair, short on the sides and longer on top, and his skin is sun-kissed, despite the fact that he lives in an underground cave.

"Pegasus! What brings you here?" He stands up, staggering forward as if his legs won't cooperate with him.

*Oh brother. He's drunk.*

He stops in front of the golden warrior and pulls him into a hug. "Glad to see you, buddy."

Pegasus becomes stiff as a board. "What's going on, Hades?"

The Underworld god eases off and frowns at him. "What? Can't I be glad to see you?"

"You've never been glad to see me since my creation."

Hades waves his hand dismissively. "Pfff. Nonsense." Finally he notices Pegasus didn't come alone. "And who did you bring with you?"

I was already tense, but now that we have the dark god's attention, I'm frozen, afraid to even breathe. Despite his level of intoxication, I feel smothered by his gaze. Talk about a powerful being. Not even Artemis felt like this.

"These are the Furies' latest victims. You've let them escape, so they're here hoping you can imprison them again."

Hades frowns, pinching his lips together. I wish Pegasus had been less blunt about his explanation.

"I had nothing to do with the Furies' escape. I wasn't even here when it happened. They had help from another god, because not even my faithful Cerberus could stop them from leaving."

"Who would help them? And to what end?" I ask.

Hades shrugs. "Don't know. But now my dear brother is pissed and has summoned me for an audience at Mount Olympus."

"Really? I didn't know about that," Pegasus replies.

"Why would you? You're only a servant."

The blond knight winces, and I feel offended on his behalf. He's been trying to help us from the get-go and without asking for anything in return. He's better than all the gods I've met so far. But I can't ruin our chances of freeing Crimson Hollow from the Furies' crutches if I antagonize Hades.

"So are you saying the Furies are stronger than you?" Tristan raises an eyebrow.

Hades's gloomy eyes sharpen for a moment. "Watch your

mouth, wolf. Those bitches aren't stronger than me. I may be drunk, but I'm still the lord of the Underworld."

*Shit. Way to go, Tristan.*

I open my mouth to try to salvage the situation when a sharp cramp robs me of breath. I bend forward, grunting.

"Red? What's the matter, love?" Sam asks, supporting me by my elbows.

"It's just a cramp. It's getting better already. I'm fine."

"You're not going into labor, are you?" Dante asks.

*Oh God, I hope not. I can't have my babies in the Underworld.* "No, of course not. It's too soon for that anyway."

I lift my head, catching Hades's gaze. His eyes are narrowed to slits, and his lips are nothing but a slash on his face. A shiver of dread runs down my spine. I don't like the calculating glint in his dark eyes one bit.

"You know what? I'm bringing you all with me," he announces.

"You don't mean that. You can't bring mortals to Mount Olympus without Zeus's permission," Pegasus retorts.

"I also wasn't supposed to see his ugly face ever again when he banished me to this forsaken place, yet here I am, summoned back to his palace in the skies."

It's impossible to miss the venom in Hades's tone.

Fuck a duck. Did we make a mistake by coming here?

"We don't nee—"

"Oh no, darling. You don't have a choice in the matter. You're all coming with me."

Before I can get another word in, the entire world goes dark and silent. I lose the sensation of my body, and I can't even scream. If I could feel my heart, it would probably be beating erratically right now.

The darkness gives way to sudden brightness. I have to shut my eyes or risk going blind. My body feels whole again, and when I sense the brightness diminish, I blink my eyes open. I'm in an atrium with a high domed ceiling supported by white Greek columns. Frescoes in soft hues adorn the walls, and somewhere nearby, someone is playing the harp. Even if those weren't enough clues to my whereabouts, the great power I sense in the air would do the trick.

This is it. Mount Olympus.

18

---

DANTE

As soon as I open my eyes, I recognize the atrium outside of Zeus's throne room. It's an old memory from my time as Artemis's wolf. I also know we need to get the hell out before Zeus discovers we're here. Pegasus wasn't kidding. Mortals aren't allowed at Mount Olympus unless Zeus wishes it so.

But first things first. I search for Red, finding her not far from me, and Sam and Tristan have already formed a protective barrier around her. I have every intention of joining them when laughter down one of the hallways reaches us, raising the small hairs on the back of my neck. My canines descend unconsciously, and a low growl comes from deep in my throat. My wolf instincts are ten times more acute here; the beast is begging to be set free. It takes great effort on my part to prevent the shift.

"Great, the welcoming committee has come to piss me off," Hades says.

"Who's coming?" Red asks, clutching at her belly.

She said she was fine, but the creases on her forehead says otherwise. She's in discomfort.

*"Red, are you okay, my love?"* I ask telepathically.

128

*"I'm fine. Well, not really. Some powerful deities are approaching."*

*"It's Apollo, Dionysius, and... ah hell, Ares,"* Sam joins the convo.

Pegasus positions himself in front of Red and my brothers, but I maintain my stance. I'm not going to cower behind Zeus's champion. But Sam and Tristan better stay by Red's side.

Apollo is the first to reach the atrium. He stops in his tracks when he notices us. He looks at me first, raising an eyebrow, before his curious gaze veers toward Pegasus and Hades, who, by some miracle, is standing next to the golden knight and thus adding another layer of protection in front of Red. I'm not sure if it's on purpose, but I'm not complaining.

"Well, well, well. Look who we got here. The black sheep of the family has returned. How have you been, Uncle?" Apollo smiles wickedly in Hades's direction.

"Spectacular. I'm surprised to see you here. Don't you have to break the hearts of innocent mortals somewhere?"

Apollo snorts. "Why do you care? Are you taking pity on the lowly peasants now that your sweet Persephone is gone?"

*Oh shit. Apollo did not just go there.* Persephone, Hades's former beloved wife, committed suicide millennia ago. I remember listening to Artemis gossip about it with Aphrodite.

Hades's face twists into an expression of fury; he's not known for reining in his temper.

"You fucking bastard!" A flaming sword appears in his hand right before he charges Apollo.

I run to Red, knowing things are about to get ugly. From the corner of my eye, I see Hades's sword fly out of his hand and land a few feet away, close to the marble steps. The fire fizzles out. I don't need to look to know who's joined us—Zeus's favorite daughter, Athena.

"What's the meaning of this?" she asks.

"Just Hades acting like a sod as usual." Apollo shrugs.

"And why are Artemis's wolves here?" She glowers in our direction.

I open my mouth to reply, but Pegasus beats me to it. "We're here because the Furies are loose and creating havoc in the mortal lands."

Athena's face remains impartial. She was always impossible to read. "How did the Furies escape your prison in the Underworld, Hades?"

"Oh fuck no. You're not laying the blame on me."

"And who else would she blame?" Ares scoffs. "You're the lord of the Underworld, aren't you?"

"It's seems someone is slacking in their job," Dionysius chimes in.

The tall golden double doors at the top of the grand stairs open outward with a bang. A six-foot-seven man with white hair and trimmed beard fills the frame. Zeus. Despite his hair coloring, his appearance is of a man in his thirties. Wearing a loose Greek-style toga with golden embellishments and a golden crown on his head, you can't mistake him for anything else but the king of Mount Olympus.

No one makes a sound as Zeus sweeps the floor with his steely gaze. When his eyes land on our party of intruders, I feel a slight tremor under my feet. Shit. He's definitely displeased with our presence here.

"Pegasus, it seems you can't stay away from those mortals." Zeus's tone is harsh.

"I was the one who brought them here," Hades declares.

The god glares at his brother through slits. "Of course you did. I want everyone in the throne room now."

"Hey, why do we have to—" Apollo starts.

"I said *now!*" Zeus's voice reverberates through the walls, hard and unyielding.

No one dares to contradict him, not even Hades.

While the gods follow Zeus to the throne room, I check on Red. She looks paler than before, but her eyes are defiant.

*"It seems everything is still the same here,"* Sam pipes up.

*"You remember them?"* Tristan asks.

*"Yeah, as soon as I got here, all my memories from my time living among the gods returned."*

*"Mine too,"* I say.

*"Everyone is an ass here. No wonder you wanted out,"* Red replies.

Pegasus turns to us. "We'd better get going. No sense in antagonizing Zeus further."

We follow him to the most lavish throne room I've ever been to. It beats Prythian's palace by a long shot. From the white marble floor with golden veins to the frescoes on the domed ceiling that seem to be in constant motion, the large room oozes power and wealth. Nothing less for the king of the gods.

Zeus is already on his throne, and next to him is Athena, always alert. Apollo, Dionysius, and Ares are on the left, and Hades is standing alone to the right. Pegasus shoots straight for the middle of the room with steady steps and shoulders squared back. I have no doubt he knows he'll be punished for assisting us again, but he doesn't seem afraid to meet his fate.

"I want an explanation for why my most trusted champion has defied my orders twice, and worse, has conspired with my pitiful brother behind my back," Zeus says coldly.

"I didn't conspire with Hades," Pegasus replies.

The dark god snorts. "You brought the wolf family to my domain and asked me to capture the Furies again. That's conspiring, in my brother's book."

"Silence!" Zeus slams his hand on the throne's arm. "You'll speak when I command you to do so."

Hades's entire body begins to shake. "You're not my fucking boss!"

"I'm your king." Zeus leans forward, body poised to strike.

"Father, if I may speak," Athena intervenes.

Zeus leans back, still glowering at Hades. But after a moment, he nods.

"I'd like to know why Artemis's wolves are here."

Before I can stop her, Red takes a step forward. "We're here because the Furies have a vendetta against Artemis and decided to take their grievances out on the inhabitants of Crimson Hollow. They've altered everyone's memories and are set on destroying my mates and me."

"And what makes you think that's our problem?" Apollo asks with an air of arrogance.

"The Furies are one of you, and they're wrecking my town. They *are* your problem."

Apollo turns his eyes to slits and flares his nostrils. Immediately, my brothers and I move closer to Red, offering her a protective barrier against the sun god.

"You're not afraid of us," Athena says.

"Oh, I am, but I don't hide in the face of danger." Red lifts her chin.

Athena keeps staring at Red for the longest time without saying a word. Not many people can withstand the goddess's stare without looking away, but not my Red. She doesn't even flinch.

"I can help you with the Furies," Athena declares suddenly.

Zeus arches his eyebrows and turns to her. "I don't remember giving you permission to interfere."

"Am I not your right hand? Don't you trust my judgment?" Athena replies calmly.

The god leans back and watches his daughter for a couple of beats during which I don't dare to breathe. Finally, he replies, "Very well."

"I know enough about deities to know you don't do anything without expecting something in return," Tristan interjects. "What's your price to help us?"

"If you pledge your sons to me, the Furies will be nothing but a nightmare."

A loud growl echoes in the room. Red steps forward, her

body shaking with anger. "You want my sons? Over my dead body."

"Red, calm down," Pegasus begs.

She whips her face to him. "Calm down, my ass. I'm not going to give my babies away."

"I asked no such thing. I have no desire to raise wolf pups. What I asked for was their allegiance."

"Meaning they would be your servants at your beck and call. No thank you," Sam retorts.

Before anyone can get another word out, a great disturbance rattles the very fabric of air surrounding us. A second later, the doors to the throne room open and in come the three bitches wrecking our lives: Tisiphone, Megaera, and Alecto. The Furies.

"So, it has come to this. The mighty Zeus has decided to bow down to the wishes of vermin," Alecto sneers.

I expect Zeus to strike the goddess with his mighty lightning fists, but all the king of gods does is stare at the blonde bitch with a bored expression in his eyes.

"You're one to talk." Apollo snorts. "Picking on defenseless humans and wolf shifters when you're too afraid to face my sister."

A golden whip erupts from the goddess's wrist, wrapping around Apollo's neck in a split second. With a hard yank, Alecto brings him to his knees while all the other gods just watch. Looking like he's struggling to breathe, Apollo grabs the whip. It melts under his touch, setting him free in an instant. In the next second, a spear made of fire appears in his hand. He launches it at Alecto, but the bitch moves out of the way and the weapon hits the far wall, burning a hole through it.

"Is Zeus just going to watch those psychopaths destroy his throne room?" Red asks, wide-eyed.

"This is entertainment to him," I say.

Megaera, the red-haired goddess, sets her eyes on us. Malice rolls out in waves from her frame. "You've proven to be more of a headache than you're worth. I'm done playing games with you." She brings her hands closer together, and from her palms, a dark energy sphere begins to form.

"Come on, we need to get out of here," Pegasus urges, but it's too late.

Megaera strikes, sending her dark energy ball in our direction. I jump over Red, bringing her down to avoid a direct hit. She falls on top of Sam, who protects her belly from hitting the hard floor. A loud explosion behind us almost makes me deaf, followed by the howling of stormy winds. No, not winds, a tornado by the sound of it.

When we begin to slide toward the noise, I look over my shoulder. The dark energy Megaera sent our way created a small black hole which is sucking us in.

"Oh my God. What's happening?" Red screams over the cacophony.

The sound of hooves on the marble floor catches my attention. Pegasus is trying to block the hole with his wings, but he'll end up getting sucked into the void if he doesn't move out of the way.

Suddenly, a piercing scream joins all the other sounds. Artemis has finally decided to join the party.

The question is, is she going to help us or watch our doom?

## 19

## RED

I can't see much with the way my mates are covering my body, but I know our situation is dire. There's no help coming from those odious gods. If I could, I'd send them straight to Hell. My wolf is churning inside of me, and the essence of the guardians has joined her too.

But besides the issue that I can't shift, my water just broke.

When the piercing scream of a woman cuts through the noise of the howling winds, I know Artemis has arrived. Her cry is of despair, that much I know. Even if I despise her, I bear her mark, and thus I have a connection with her.

I scrunch my face and bite the inside of my cheek when a contraction comes through. It doesn't last long, but the pain is enough to make me see stars.

Fuck a duck. This is just the beginning.

The wind stops suddenly, and finally my mates give me some breathing room. Leaning on one elbow, I lift my head in time to see Artemis pierce Alecto's shoulder with one of her arrows. The other two Furies give a battle cry and advance toward the redheaded goddess, but Apollo and Ares block their way, engaging them in battle.

Another contraction comes along, so strong that I can't help but cry out loud.

"Red? What's happening?" Sam is in front of me in an instant.

"Oh hell. What's that puddle under you?" Tristan asks

"My water… broke. The… babies are… coming," I grit out.

"No, you can't have them here. We need to go back to Crimson Hollow," Sam replies.

I yell when another painful contraction robs me of air. I knew labor pains were the worst, but I had no idea they were this bad. It's hell. The sound of battle is still going on in the background, but the world could be ending and it wouldn't matter to me.

"Sending you back to Crimson Hollow right now is too risky." Pegasus reappears before me in his human form.

"Riskier than Red having our babies in the middle of a fight between gods?" Tristan shouts.

"Damn it! It's too soon." Dante rubs his face, not hiding his worry.

"Not you… too," I grunt. "I need… someone to… remain calm."

Suddenly, everything becomes eerily quiet, and time seems to be going in slow motion. The strange effect only lasts a couple of seconds, but when things returned to normal, Zeus is standing, and in his hand, he has a staff that's glowing bright blue, just like his eyes.

The Furies are facedown on the floor with their hands behind their backs. As far as I can tell, nothing is keeping them there, at least nothing visible to the naked eye. But I have no doubt that Zeus is responsible for it.

"I've had enough of this. Artemis, you started this war. You shall end it someplace else."

"You want me to fight them alone?" She raises both eyebrows.

"You knew the consequences when you connived with my brother to have them locked away. Now deal with it."

Artemis opens her mouth to reply, but another scream escapes my lips. Fuck, now they're all looking at me. I wish I could suffer in silence.

"What fresh hell is this?" Hades asks.

"She's in labor," Pegasus replies. "Artemis, she needs you."

"I… don't… need her." I glower in the goddess's direction.

"Oh shit! Is that blood?" Sam asks.

Artemis appears by my side in the blink of an eye. "Your babies are in distress."

"How do you know?" Tristan watches her suspiciously.

"I'm the goddess of childbirth, mongrel."

Tristan peels his lips back and growls in her direction, but Dante puts a hand on his arm and keeps him in place. "She's not wrong. This birth is premature and risky for Red and the babies. Artemis can help."

"I don't… want… ugh!" I roll onto my back and close my eyes. The contractions are coming one after another and lasting much longer.

"Can't you help her with the pain?" Sam asks.

"I could, but I need Red to feel everything. Her reaction will help me assess the situation."

I don't believe a word coming out of her mouth. She doesn't want to take away the pain because she's enjoying watching me suffer. But I'm not going to beg. I'll push through this.

"So we can go now? I have no desire to watch a she-wolf pop a litter out of her," Hades says.

I'd tell him to fuck himself if I could say anything right now. I hear a tear, and then my leggings are coming off. Great, now I'm exposed to all these asshole gods. I'm used to being naked in front of strangers, but I don't want an audience of hateful gods while I have my babies. I want to share this special moment with my mates only.

Artemis spreads my legs and positions herself in front of me. "We need to get these babies out. I need you to start pushing hard."

Dante kneels next to Artemis while Tristan and Sam hold each of my hands.

"Come on, baby. You can do this," Sam says.

My reply is a grunt, because another contraction is coming and I can't focus on anything besides the pain.

Pegasus, back in horse form, steps in front of me and spreads his wings, blocking the other gods' view.

"Oh come on. Is that really necessary?" Dionysius asks.

"She's in a lot of distress. She doesn't need four buffoons ogling her on top of it," Athena retorts.

Those are the last words I hear from the group of gods in the room. Artemis is the only one commanding my attention now.

I'm not sure how long it takes for the first baby to come out, but when I hear the shrill cry of a newborn, tears of joy roll down my cheeks.

"Oh my God. He's beautiful, my love." Dante cradles our son in his arms.

"Can I see him?" I ask.

"Not right now, girl. You still have two more babies to go," Artemis cuts in like a blunt knife.

The contractions keep coming, and it's not long before the second baby is born.

"It's another boy," Artemis announces before she hands him to Tristan's waiting arms.

"He's perfect," he coos.

"Okay, one more to go. You can do this, Red," Artemis says.

Her encouragement is a surprise, but I'm too tired to find out if she means it or not. The contractions are more violent now, and the pain is so excruciating, it's a miracle I haven't passed out yet. But no matter how hard I push, the baby won't come out.

"This isn't right," Artemis mutters, driving a spike through my heart.

"What's the matter?" I ask.

She doesn't answer, just keeps staring at my belly with her eyebrows furrowed.

A cackle from outside the perimeter makes my blood run cold. "She won't tell you, but we will," one of the Furies says.

"What's wrong with my baby!" I ask Artemis again.

"Come down, love. Don't listen to those shrews," Sam replies.

"Your baby is dead," the Fury continues.

"Silence!" Athena yells, followed by a grunt.

I don't know what's happening out there, but the Fury managed to put fear in my heart.

"She's lying, right? Tell me she's lying," Sam begs Artemis.

The goddess won't make eye contact with anyone, but once I turn my attention to Dante, my heart stops beating. His solemn expression is clue enough that something terrible has happened.

"Please, Dante. Tell me she's lying." I begin to cry.

Artemis places her hand on my belly and reaches inside of me with the other. I cry out when she pulls something out of me slowly. My baby girl. Only there's no crying.

Dante looks at her tiny, still body and lets out a sob. "No...."

"Give me the girl," Athena commands, standing tall next to Artemis. I didn't even see her approach.

"No, I want to hold her," I say.

Artemis ignores my pleas and hands my daughter to the goddess of warfare. Pegasus returns to his human form and stands next to her, his eyes intent.

"What are you going to do?" he asks.

Athena places her hand on my baby's chest, and a glowing light forms around her small body. I don't dare to breathe until I see her arms move. The light fades away, and my baby begins to cry in earnest. Athena smiles, seemingly enamored with my daughter. I can never repay her for bringing her back to me, but I'm also terrified of what her act of kindness means.

"Can I have her?" I ask.

The goddess looks at me and nods. When she places my little girl in my arms, I'm overcome with joy and love.

"Thank you," I breathe.

"She's a fighter. She had to live."

"No! That wasn't supposed to happen," Alecto breaks free from her invisible holding, and in the blink of an eye, she launches Athena's own spear at her.

It goes straight through the warrior goddess's chest. She glances down, surprised to see the weapon embedded in her, before her knees give out and she collapses on the floor.

"You filthy cunt!" Zeus roars, creating a vortex of the most vicious storm I've ever seen. It covers the Furies, savage and merciless, before it rushes them out of the throne room to who knows where.

No one speaks for several beats. I still can't believe this happened. How did Alecto manage to break free from Zeus's hold? Why did Athena leave her spear within the Fury's reach? But all those questions remain stuck in my throat. Zeus is coming in our direction, power crackling. I clutch my baby girl closer to my chest, terrified of what he's going to do us.

He crouches next to Athena's body and touches her hair. "My beautiful daughter. Why did it have to be you?"

My own daughter begins to cry in earnest, drawing Zeus's attention to us. He turns, leveling me with the coldest glare. "I should end you for the disgrace you brought to my house. But my daughter chose to bestow life upon your offspring for a reason. Be eternally grateful for that."

"I am," I croak.

"That's not enough." Zeus unfurls from his crouch. "You'll pledge her and your sons to Athena."

I swallow the huge lump in my throat. That's the last thing I want for my babies, to be tied to a god, even if it's a dead one. But looking at the solemn expression on my mates' faces and then catching the slight nod from Pegasus, I know I don't have a choice.

"Yes, I'll pledge my sons and daughter to Athena," I say with a heavy heart.

Zeus flicks his wrist, and three light blue strings float from it. They wrap around my sons' and daughter's wrists before disappearing.

"So it is done," he declares.

2 0

---

RED

One moment I'm staring at Zeus's hard face, and in the next I'm back home, alone in my room, without my babies or my mates. Desperation seizes me. Like a madwoman, I burst through the door.

"Dante! Sam! Tristan!" I scream from the top of my lungs.

The door to the nursery opens and out they come, each holding a baby in their arms. I stop in my tracks, but my heart is still beating at warp speed.

"We're here, baby." Sam smiles at me.

I place a hand over my chest. "I was so scared Zeus had lied and taken my babies away."

"No he didn't." Dante stops next to me, holding our daughter. She's sound asleep and so beautiful. A lump gets stuck in my throat and tears fill my eyes.

"How can you be back on your feet after that ordeal?" Tristan inspects me from head to toe.

It's then that I realize I not only feel great, but my body is back to how it was pre-pregnancy. And most importantly, I'm fully clothed.

"I think Zeus did more than just bring us back," I reply.

"Do you think everything has returned to normal?" Sam stares at me with a little apprehension in his eyes.

"The nursery has, and Zeus dealt with those b—with the Furies," Tristan replies.

"They can't understand you yet." I smile at this attempt to cover the swear word.

"I know, but soon they will. We have to practice. Do you want to hold him?" He comes closer.

"We need to give them names," Dante says.

"I know. How about naming one of the boys after your father?" I ask.

My mates trade a glance among themselves, and I catch the unspoken message. "What?"

"We thought about it, but we think it might make Mom more sad than happy. I don't think she's recovered completely from his death."

"Oh, okay." I glance at my son, so pink and chubby with a hint of blond hair on his head. "You look like a Jude to me."

"Ugh, not Jude," Sam whines.

But the baby smiles in his sleep. "Shush, he likes it," I say.

"I like Jude," Tristan replies.

"Me too," Dante chimes in.

"Fine, you can name him Jude, but then I get to pick the name of this little fella here." Sam kisses the top of his head.

I narrow my eyes. "Only if it's not a ridiculous name."

"He looks like... Lochie." Sam smiles cheekily, showing his adorable dimples.

"You're not naming him after a Marvel character," I grumble.

"Not Loki with a K, L-O-C-H-I-E," Sam replies.

"Potato, potahto. It sounds exactly the same," Tristan retorts.

"Hmm, I don't know. Loki was a Norse god. It would be a snub to the Greek gods if we named him after such an infamous Norse deity," Dante replies.

"Exactly." Sam grins victoriously.

"I suppose it's not a bad name," I relent.

"All right. Lochie Wolfe it is." Sam peers down at our son with a radiant smile.

"How about our little girl? What are we going to call her?" Tristan asks.

I grin, knowing exactly the perfect name for her. "Diana."

"You know Diana is the Roman name for Artemis, right?" Dante says.

"I know. A part of me wants to keep hating her, but she *did* come to help us in the end. I don't think the babies or I would have survived if she hadn't appeared at the last minute."

"I can't argue with that logic. And also, after what you went through to bring them to the world, you could name her Merengue if you wanted to." Tristan smirks.

I try to glower, but the corners of my lips twitch up, giving me away.

"So it's settled, then. Diana, Jude, and Lochie. Welcome to the family," Sam declares.

"Red! Are you there?" Kenya's loud voice booms from the entry hall.

In unison, our daughter and sons begin to cry in earnest.

"Nice job, Kenya," Sam mutters.

"Oh my God! Do I hear babies?" Her voice is getting closer. Soon she reaches the landing of the second floor, breathless and disheveled.

"Hi." I turn to her

"Red, oh my God. You're okay." Her eyes are round and bright as she approaches. "When did this happen?"

"When we were forced to attend a meeting at Mount Olympus," I reply.

"Holy fucking shit. You went to Mount Olympus? Who did you see?"

"Hey, language," Tristan complains.

"Bite me, wolf boy. After the hellish night I just had, I can curse as much as I want to. Besides, the babies can't understand anything."

"What's the last thing you remember?" I ask.

"Getting turned into a miniature toy. Then I woke up in my bed, in PJs, as if the whole thing had been a nightmare. But it happened, right? The Furies were really here wreaking havoc."

"Yes, but Zeus took care of them," I say.

"He did? Oh my God. I can't believe you met him. Who else was there?"

"We had the displeasure of meeting Athena, Apollo, Hades, Ares, and Dionysius," Tristan sneers.

"Really? Wow, I would have loved to be there."

"No you wouldn't," the four of us say at the same time.

"Crap on toast. What happened to Zeke and Billy?" I ask.

"I just saw Billy heading to class. He seemed normal."

"He didn't say anything to you?" I watch her closely.

"No. Why? Should he?"

"Maybe he doesn't remember going to the Wastelands," Dante muses. "If Zeus fixed everyone's memories, then it's like last night never happened."

"We should call the bakery to make sure Zeke is okay."

"So your babies were born at Mount Olympus?" Kenya peers down at Jude.

"Yeah, in Zeus's throne room to be exact," I say.

"So they're Olympians." She grins at me.

"Ugh, I hadn't thought of that."

"They're Wolfe, and that's all that matters," Tristan declares with a lift of his chin.

Indeed, that's all that matters—for now anyway. Who knows when Zeus will come back to impose the pledge I was forced to make.

SIX MONTHS LATER...

I take my time in the shower, enjoying the moment of peace. Being a mom of three active and loud babies has taken every single waking moment of my life in the past six months, even with my mates' help. I'm sleep deprived and tired as hell, but I wouldn't trade my life right now for anything in the world. I didn't know I was capable of loving someone as fiercely and unconditionally as I love Diana, Lochie, and Jude.

But finally, I was able to carve up an entire afternoon sans kids thanks to Billy and Nadine, who volunteered to babysit with Dr. Mervina's supervision. Not that I don't trust the teens, but three babies are a lot of responsibility.

I'm supposed to meet with Kenya, but when I get out of the bathroom, a find a very naked Sam in our bed. He has a red rose in his hand and a very obvious erection. Heat surges straight from core, and my appointment with Kenya is forgotten.

"Hello, gorgeous. I've been waiting for you."

"What are you doing here? I thought you were meeting with the guys?" I step closer to the bed, unable to ignore the pull.

I was afraid that after the babies were born, my libido would plummet. But I still yearn for my mates with as much fervor as before. I'm glad that wolf shifters can only conceive during heat, because with how hard we practice making babies, I'd be knocked up again by now.

"I heard Billy and Nadine are playing house with the kids, so I postponed my meeting with my bandmates." His eyes travel the length of my body, making me even hotter. "Whatcha got under that towel, love?"

"Wouldn't you like to know?" I raise an eyebrow.

Sam sits at the edge of the bed and reaches for me. "Yes, I'd very much like to know." He glides the rose over the swell of my breasts and caresses my leg with his free hand, moving up until he reaches the apex of my thighs.

I close my eyes and let out a moan. When a low growl sounds in the room, I know it didn't come from Sam. Tristan is here. The bedroom door closes with a soft click. I glance in his direction, finding him already loosening his tie. Damn, he's sexy.

Sam's fingers sweep over my clit, making me focus on him again. "It's seems it's a double treat afternoon delight."

My lips curl into a grin. "No, it's a triple treat."

Dante comes into the room in the next second. I sensed him when he came bursting through the manor's front door.

"Did I miss anything?" he asks.

"As you can see, I'm still wrapped in my towel, so no," I reply.

Tristan kisses my neck, and with a yank, the towel drops to the floor. "Problem solved," he whispers in my ear, making goose bumps run down my arm.

Sam doesn't waste any time. He nudges my legs apart and sweeps his tongue across my clit. I throw my head back and close my eyes, trying to remain standing. Tristan continues to kiss my neck while playing with a breast. Dante latches onto my other nipple, running circles around the tight nub until my head feels light. I grab a fistful of Sam's hair and urge him to lick faster. My mates have turned me into a veritable nymphomaniac, and I'm totally okay with it.

I'm about to come when Sam pulls back, and Dante and Tristan do the same.

"Why did you stop?" I ask.

"Switch," Sam replies with a wicked smile.

He scooches back, leaving room for Dante, Tristan, and I to join him in bed. They flip me on my back, and now it's Tristan between my legs, sucking and fucking me with his fingers. I arch my back, stretching my arms toward Sam and Dante, who are on each side of me. I can't simply receive and not give back, so I wrap my fingers around their lengths and have my fun with them.

Time seems to not have any meaning as I get lost in the lust-infused fog of mating. With each stroke of Tristan's tongue against my clit, I move an inch closer to the edge. But like Sam did before, he stops right before I take the plunge.

"Oh come on," I whine.

"Switch" is his reply.

I swear to God, they're doing this on purpose to torture me. I'm so horny right now that a hot breath near my pussy would probably shatter me into pieces. But I too can play this game. Instead of letting Dante take Tristan's place, I get on my knees and push him on his back.

"Red, what are—" His reply is cut short when I straddle him, bringing his cock to my entrance.

"It's my time to lead." I lower myself, and Dante slides in. He lets out a growl, grabbing my hips. Naturally, he tries to set the pace, but I'm an alpha too, so I grab his wrists and take control of the situation. "I said I've got this. Are you going to behave?"

"Yes," he breathes.

"Good." I lift my face to Tristan and Sam, who are busy stroking themselves. "Come here, you two."

They surround me, showering me with kisses and caresses. I replace their hands on their cocks with mine while I ride Dante. It takes a few seconds to find my rhythm, but when I do, there's no stopping me. No more switching until I say so. When Dante gets even larger inside of me, I increase my pace, knowing he's just as close to an orgasm as I am. Tristan's and Sam's grunts make me pump their shafts faster as well. They come almost at the same time, and not much later, I'm screaming in unison with Dante.

My entire body shakes as I ride my climax. It seems to me the more often we do it, the longer they last. Not that I'm complaining. I don't stop moving my hips until I'm completely boneless, and then I slide off Dante in a not so graceful way and close my eyes.

Three pairs of arms hug me, forming a warm cocoon of bliss. I refuse to move, even when I hear my phone ring on the nightstand. It's Kenya's signature ringtone, so I let it go to voice mail. I'll ask for forgiveness later. I've more than earned every precious moment with my mates, and this is a right I'll never give up.

*** ALMOST THE END. THE NEXT CHAPTER CONTAINS A SMALL CLIFFHANGER FOR THE WOLVES OF CRIMSON HOLLOW SPIN-OFF SERIES. ***

## 21

RED

I don't wake up from my post-sex nap until much later. It's already past six in the evening, and the loud voices of visitors are what finally jar me awake. I nudge the guys so I can lean on my elbows.

"What time is it?" Dante asks with a yawn.

"Ten past six. It sounds like we have company," I reply.

"Oh yeah. Mom invited some friends over for cake," Tristan replies.

"Cake? Are we celebrating something?"

"The triplets' six-month birthday," Sam replies.

I furrow my brow. "I didn't know we were doing that."

"It was Zeke's idea." Sam chuckles.

I roll my eyes. "Of course it was. He's just trying to get business for his bakery."

Despite that, the prospect of a birthday cake from the imp's establishment is enough for me to get going. I push Tristan out of the way and run to the shower. My mates follow me a few minutes later, but I jump out before they can corner me there. It'll only lead to more sex, and it would be rude to leave our guests waiting. Plus, I've already pissed off Kenya enough for one day.

I'm the first one down, and of course, the first person I see is her. She crosses her arms and tries to level me with a glare.

"You have some explanation to do, Red."

"I'm sorry. Something came up." I avoid her gaze.

"Something, right. Just say you stood me up for a sausage party."

"What sausage party? Are we having hot dogs?" Billy comes in carrying Jude in his arms. Nadine follows him with Lochie.

She gives him a droll stare before shaking her head.

"Red had some earlier." Kenya smirks at me.

Nadine pretends to be gagging before she goes to sit by Leo, Jared, and Armand in the living room.

I look around. "Who has Diana now?"

"Oh, she's outside with Uncle Zeke," Billy replies.

"She's alone with him?" I ask, my voice sounding a little shrilly.

"Why are you freaking out, Red? Zeke is harmless." Kenya shrugs.

I don't know why I'm nervous all of a sudden, so instead of answering her, I stride out of the manor. Zeke is standing right in front of the house, but he doesn't have Diana. She's in the arms of a familiar tall blond golden knight. Pegasus.

My heart skips a beat before jumping up to my throat.

"What are you doing here?" I ask.

He looks at me, his face serene for once. I guess when you're not worried about psycho deities, it's easy to feel relaxed. Too bad I don't share his sentiment.

"Hi, Red. How have you been?" He gives me a small smile

"Fine until you showed up here." I take Diana from his arms and she immediately begins to cry. Little traitor.

The grin vanishes from his face. "I'm sorry if my presence disturbs you. It wasn't my intention."

"You couldn't guess that after everything I went through, I'd want my distance from your kind?"

"I suppose I should have guessed as much."

"Come on, Red. Don't you think you're being a little harsh with Pegasus? If it weren't for him, the Furies would have gotten away with their revenge," Zeke interjects.

I glower at the imp, but I can't fault his logic. Shit. I *am* being unfair.

I let out a sigh. "I'm sorry. Did you just come by to pay a social visit?"

Heat rushes to his cheeks. He rubs the back of his neck and says, "No, actually I came here because Zeus sent me."

My blood runs cold. That's it. The king of Olympus has sent his champion to take my babies away. I clutch Diana closer to my chest, taking a step back for good measure.

"Why?" I ask.

"I've been assigned to be your children's guardian."

"What?" I squeak.

"That's interesting." Zeke rubs his chin.

"You pledged them in service to Athena. Zeus wants to make sure nothing happens to them."

"Are they in danger?" Zeke asks.

"Not right now. But that might not last. Athena had many enemies, and baby Diana bears her mark."

"Come again?" I say.

"When Athena brought your baby back to life, she marked her. Just like you have the mark of Artemis, Diana has the mark of Athena."

"Does that mean she'll have special powers?" I glance at my baby's chubby face, wishing she could live a normal shifter life.

"Possibly. But you don't see that as a blessing, do you?"

I glare at Pegasus. "No, I don't. Being a wolf is enough." A hint of regret flashes in the champion's eyes, sending alarms through my head. "What is it?"

"You haven't realized it yet. Diana is not a wolf shifter."

"What? Nonsense. Of course she is."

I sense Zeke's intense stare in my direction. No, not my direction. Diana's.

"I'll be damned. I can't believe I missed that," he mutters.

"Athena could only resuscitate your baby's human side. Unfortunately, the wolf died."

I hug my baby tighter while fighting back the tears. "No."

"Red?" Dante calls my name.

A second later, all my mates are running to me.

"Red, what's wrong?" Sam asks me.

"What are you doing here? What did you do to Red?" Tristan gets into Pegasus's personal space.

"Guys, calm down." Zeke pulls Tristan back.

The tears are falling freely now. As if knowing how broken-hearted I am, Diana places her chubby hand on my face.

"Mama," she says for the first time.

"Oh my God. Did she just say 'mama'?" Sam moves closer.

"Yes." I laugh. "Yes, she did. Hello, darling. That's me, your mama."

Diana giggles in delight, melting my heart.

"Why were you crying, love?" Dante asks.

I shake my head. "It's not that important. I'll tell you later."

Dante frowns slightly, but he doesn't push it. I'll tell them once the party is over. I don't want to sour everyone's mood now.

"Come on, let's go back inside. There's nothing a good slice of cake can't fix," I say.

"Oh, especially if they're one of mine." Zeke winks at me.

We all walk toward the door, but Pegasus doesn't follow. I look over my shoulder. "You're not coming?"

"Wait, are you inviting him?" Tristan asks.

"Sure, why not?"

Pegasus twists his face into an expression I can only guess is discomfort. If he's feeling awkward now, wait until Kenya sets her eyes on him.

---

DANTE

The party is over, the babies are sleeping, and we're back in our room. I know the news Red needs to tell us. It's hard keeping a straight face when she reveals Diana isn't a wolf shifter. I suspected as much as soon as we returned home from Mount Olympus. But it was only when Mom examined her that my suspicions were confirmed. I couldn't tell Red or my brothers. They would be devastated, especially Red. So I waited for the best opportunity to tell them, but Pegasus beat me to it.

"Are you sure that winged horse was telling the truth?" Sam asks.

"Why would he lie?" Red retorts.

"He's not lying," I say. "Mom and I have known about Diana since she came home."

"What? You knew all this time and didn't tell us?" Tristan raises his voice.

"I'm sorry. I didn't have the heart to tell you then. And the longer I waited, the harder it became to come clean." I turn to Red. "Please forgive me, my love. I was only trying to protect you."

She closes her eyes for a moment before looking at me again. "As much as I hate that you kept such a huge secret from us, I can't stay mad at you."

I let out a breath of relief. "Thank you. You don't know how much this secret weighed on me."

Tristan rubs his face and looks away. "Life is going to be so hard for our little girl."

"Only if we let it be," Red says. "We're much more involved with the rest of the community now. She won't grow up among wolves only. She'll be okay."

"How about this deal of her having the mark of Athena. That doesn't worry you?" Sam asks.

Red raises her chin, her face a mask of determination. "At first, yes, but not anymore. I think Athena knew exactly what she was doing. Diana was born to be a warrior, and the goddess gave her the tools. Our baby girl will be fine."

"And until she learns how to use those tools, we'll be there to protect her," Tristan adds.

"I feel sorry for whoever tries to harm any of our kids." Sam cracks his knuckles.

Red glows for a moment, but since neither Sam nor Tristan comment on it, I think I'm the only one who sees it.

The guardians are still with her.

I open my mouth to reply, but one of the babies starts to cry, and a second later, all three are bawling.

"Our grown-up time is up." Red heads for the door.

"I hope not for the rest of the evening. I could use some more grown-up time." Sam hugs Red from behind and kisses her shoulder.

"Can't you get your mind out of the gutter for one second?" Tristan grumbles.

I take a step forward to follow them when, from the corner of my eye, I catch a shimmering apparition in the corner of the room. The hairs on the back of my neck stand on end as I turn.

"Athena? What are you doing here?" I ask the ghost of the goddess.

"Oh, Dante. I never left and you know it."

I swallow the lump in my throat.

"You should have told them the whole truth," she continues.

"What whole truth?" I curl my hands into fists.

"That Diana is me."

***

Thank you for reading Red's story.
I'm not quite ready to leave this world yet. If you feel the same way, pre-order *A Touch of Hades*, the first book in my new series *Gods After Dark: Hades & Persephone*.

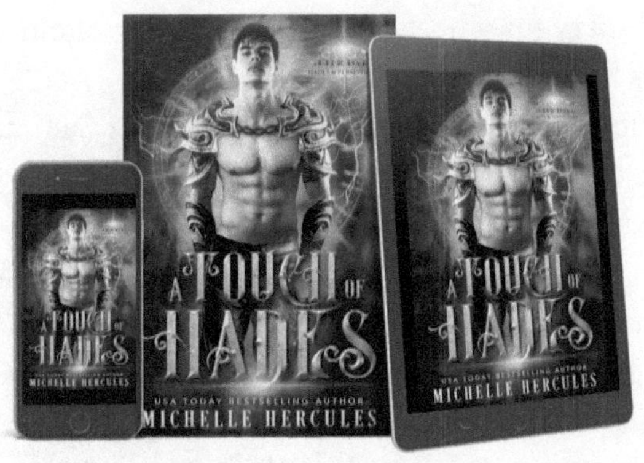

I've known the Olympian gods were real my entire life. I was born right in the middle of Zeus's throne room, after all. But as the only non-supernatural being in my family, I was resigned to live a normal life.

Until Infuriatingly cocky and impossibly handsome Hades drags me to a world of rage and fire. I hate him on sight.

I'm in a parallel dimension, and in this universe, the foulest creatures and monsters are out, terrorizing humanity.

I'm the only one who can send them back to where they belong.

There's only one problem. To do that, I must win the ultimate weapon, Athena's golden armor, which is now a prize in a deadly tournament.

And guess who volunteered to be my trainer? Hades, naturally. In this do-or-die situation, failure is not an option. Falling for Hades' charm isn't either. But what if I'm more than just his champion? What if I'm his destiny?

**Pre-order A TOUCH OF HADES now!**

# ABOUT THE AUTHOR

*USA Today* Bestselling Author Michelle Hercules always knew creative arts were her calling but not in a million years did she think she would become an author. With a background in fashion design she thought she would follow that path. But one day, out of the blue, she had an idea for a book. One page turned into ten pages, ten pages turned into a hundred, and before she knew, her first novel, The Prophecy of Arcadia, was born.

Michelle Hercules resides in Florida with her husband and daughter. She is currently working on the *Blueblood Vampires* series and the *Rebels of Rushmore* series.

**Join Michelle's Readers' Group:**
https://www.facebook.com/groups/mhsoars

*Connect with Michelle Hercules:*
www.michellehercules.com
books@mhsoars.com